APLEY TOWERS

Good Enough

Myra King

Sweet Cherry
Publishing

Sweet Cherry
Publishing

Published by Sweet Cherry Publishing Limited
Unit E, Vulcan Business Complex
Vulcan Road
Leicester, LE5 3EB
United Kingdom

www.sweetcherrypublishing.com

First published in the UK in 2016
ISBN: 978-1-78226-282-4

Illustrations © Creative Books
Illustrated by Subrata Mahajan
Cover design and illustration by Andrew Davis

Apley Towers: Good Enough

The right of Myra King to be identified as
the author of this work has been asserted by her in
accordance with the Copyright, Designs and
Patents Act 1988.

Printed and bound by Thomson Press (India) Limited.

For my grandmothers:
Maisie Pepler - who gave me her looks, her talent, and her country.
And Alice Hörstmann - who gave me everything else.

"The moment you doubt whether you can fly,
You cease forever to be able to do it."
- J. M. Barrie

❧ One ❧

The large trucks rumbled down the street. Every resident of Port St. Christopher came to a stop and stared. It was a strange procession, although it was one the truck drivers were used to. Mothers and their children stared in wonder as each heavily laden truck drove by. Shop assistants left their posts and stood in doorways to catch a glimpse. Groups of teenagers stared with barely concealed excitement: they finally had something new to complain about.

Once all the trucks had passed and the street was once again home to more normal traffic, a small child cried out the thought on everyone's mind.

"The fair is coming!"

For one brief, beautiful moment, the residents of Port St. Christopher were in harmony. For one brief moment they all cheered for the trucks and what they brought.

Trixie King hopped back on her bike and cycled as

quickly as she could to the Apley Towers stables.

"The fair is coming! The fair is coming!" she cried to every rider she passed on the dirt path that ran between the stable and its neighbour.

"The fair is coming!" she cried to riders walking to rival stables.

"The fair is coming!" she cried to anyone who would listen.

"Does it not come every year at the exact same time? Should you not be used to it by now? Has the novelty not worn off after ten years?"

Trixie looked at the man who had just spoken. Mr Henry was the stuff of legend around Apley Towers; he was the worst type of person to live next to a riding school. He hated children, he hated horses, and if you believed the rumours, he believed his close proximity to both was destroying his love of life.

Trixie didn't believe the rumours. Whatever had happened to destroy old man Henry's love of life must have happened a few minutes after his birth. She watched as he used rusted hedge clippers to attack a plant that was settling down for winter.

She smiled at him and followed two riders into Apley Towers.

"What was that about?" one of the riders turned in their saddle to ask.

Trixie looked up and whispered, "Just a run-in with the Grim Reaper."

Trixie shook her head angrily and parked her bike in the metal slots. She walked over to the two riders as they dismounted. The one on the left who had spoken was Angela May, one of Trixie's closest friends. She watched Angela pat Dawn, her horse, and wave goodbye to the other rider. She walked off leaving Trixie to stare at a beautiful grey Lipizzaner and her brown-haired owner.

"Hi Russell."

"Hello," he said and pulled a burr from Vanity Fair's mane, "don't worry about old man Henry, he has been standing in the sunlight for too long. It can't be good for his vampire skin."

"Last week he was a goblin, now you are saying that he is a vampire. What is he going to be next week?"

"Moved back to England?"

"Is that where he's from?" she asked as they began walking to the stalls.

"Yeah, can't you hear his accent?"

"I'm too busy trying not to get grumpy old man cooties to pay attention to his accent."

"Have you noticed how many British people live in Port St. Christopher?" Russell asked with big eyes, "We might as well not even be living in South Africa."

"Maybe it is a plot to overthrow us. Led by old man Henry."

The two turned to look in the direction of the Henry household. They looked at each other and hurried away.

"Miss Kaela Willoughby."

Kaela smiled and turned to look at the stable owner, "Ms Wendy Oberon."

"I need you to do me a favour. I know you love riding Quiet Fire, but you are the only person not scared to ride Spirit."

"You want me to ride Spirit in the lesson?"

"Please. I need to start getting this horse trained for competitions."

Kaela nodded. Wendy looked relieved.

"He still needs a lot of patience and training. Take it easy with him," Wendy said as she walked away.

By the time Kaela had Spirit tacked up and in the ring, she wished she had stretched more before mounting him. Quiet Fire, the horse Kaela usually rode, was bigger than Spirit but his movements were far gentler. Kaela knew that once in his saddle, she would almost always stay. With Spirit, Kaela had to use her legs and balance herself far more than she ever had before.

In front of her, Trixie on her own horse Siren put everyone to shame.

"Riding like a pro today, Trix!" Wendy called.

"Thank you."

Kaela knew Trixie had been putting in as many extra hours as she could to get Siren up to standard in dressage. It showed. Kaela, on the other hand, hated dressage and

9

couldn't wait for the first thirty minutes of the lesson to be over and done with.

"When is the next show jumping competition?" Emily, another rider, asked.

"At the end of the month. It's also a dressage competition. Bella and Trixie, I've already entered both of you. Russell, can you handle dressage?"

"Yes."

"Okay, you three are representing Apley. We have never taken home a ribbon in intermediate dressage. So I'm *hoping* one of you will break that habit."

"Good thing dressage is extremely easy then, huh?" Trixie said, sarcastically.

"Emily, Jasmyn, Russell and Kaela, I'm expecting at least three ribbons for jumping. Apley has never walked away with less than three ribbons in jumping."

"No pressure then," joked Jasmyn.

"Who am I riding?" Kaela asked.

Wendy pursed her lips and frowned, "Let's decide closer to the time. Spirit may not be ready."

Kaela frowned down at the horse. He was the only stallion at Apley, meaning that he was full of hormones and could be unpredictable. Was a show jumping competition really a good idea?

Or did Kaela just not want to lose her opportunity to compete and win with her tried and tested favourite, Quiet Fire?

Angela packed all her tack away, gave her horses their last pat of the day, and walked toward the car park where her mom was waiting. Wendy was already there, chatting to Gwendolyn May.

"Just the woman I want to see," Wendy said as Angela walked up.

"Good thing we both happen to be at this stable then."

Wendy smiled at her, "Do you know what a Superius test is?"

Angela nodded, "It's a height competition. The jump is set at a certain height, and each time you clear it they raise the jump by three inches and keep raising it until you can't jump it. Apparently it gets to impossible heights."

"Well, Equestrian International is doing one of these for the very first time. It is not part of the Season, and they have requested that each stable only enter one rider."

"And I'm your one rider?"

"If you want to be."

"Of course, but don't you think Dawn will be at a disadvantage by being so small?" Angela asked.

"No, that horse has invisible wings."

"I agree," Angela said with a proud smile.

Wendy unfolded a small piece of paper and handed it over to Angela.

"Next weekend there is a dressage show for the Season.

The weekend after is meant to be a break, so that is when they are holding the Superius competition. They've pushed the actual break to the next weekend, and that is when Pignut Spinney will host their own competition. Are you up to competing three weekends in a row?"

"Professional horse riders compete for forty-two weekends of the year. It'll be good practice for me."

Wendy nodded, "Good way to look at it."

As Angela stared at the schedule, a flutter of fear danced its way across her stomach.

Could she possibly do this without breaking down in exhaustion?

She would have to.

❧ Two ❧

"Welcome to the first Lost Kodas meeting of the month of June," Kaela said with a smile as she stared into the camera on her father's computer.

The other members of The Lost Kodas stared back at her from three separate screens. The only one sitting in sunlight was Phoenix White Feather, the Canadian member of their club.

"We have quite a hectic month ahead of us: a competition on nearly every weekend, a very serious date, and an extremely serious play. Firstly, let's discuss these competitions."

Kaela ruffled through her blank pages, trying to appear professional. The other girls laughed.

"Anybody else notice that the youngest member is the one that rules the roost?" Phoenix asked.

"That's because I am the founder."

"I'm the founder of Chinese Food Friday, but you seem

to have overthrown that as well," Trixie teased.

"It's not about overthrowing, it's about proper management."

"Oh, my mistake," Trixie said with a wave of her hand.

"Okay, back to the meeting. Angela, tell us about this Superius test."

Angela quickly explained the principles of the unusual competition.

"But Dawn is tiny," Trixie said.

"I'm not entering to win," Angela said, "the more competitions I do, the better it is for my career. If Dawn gets knocked out in the first round, I can still say I have competed in a Superius test."

"We are coming to watch," Kaela said.

"Of course you are."

"Okay, and then the next competition is Pignut Spinney. Trix, are you going to do any jumping?" Kaela asked.

"Nope. My horse, my rules: I am only doing dressage."

If only we were all so free, Kaela thought.

She didn't even know which horse she would be riding.

"And next order of business, the big date," Kaela said and wiggled her eyebrows up and down.

"Oh, the date," Phoenix laughed.

"The *date,*" Angela teased.

Trixie rolled her eyes, "You three need lives."

"Hey, it isn't every day that the stable hottie promises to give you the stars."

14

"He is taking me to the planetarium. He is hardly giving me actual stars."

"You are the most unromantic person on earth," Phoenix said, "and that's saying something, because I thought I was."

"We will have a meeting the day after the date to get all the details," Kaela said.

"Wild horses couldn't drag the details from me," replied Trixie.

"Is that a challenge?" Kaela asked, raising an eyebrow, "I know a bunch of wild horses."

"Speaking of which, why were you riding the demon stallion?" Angela asked.

"Wendy is trying to get him ready for competitions."

Trixie's eyes widened, "You are competing with *him* at Pignut Spinney?"

Kaela shrugged, "I don't know yet. Not even Wendy knows."

"Well that sucks," Angela said. "It's high time you got your own horse."

Kaela shrugged, she wasn't quite sure how she felt about it all just yet.

"Okay, last order of business: the play."

Angela and Trixie cheered. Phoenix smiled nervously.

"How long till it opens?" Kaela asked.

"Three weeks."

"Fingers crossed nothing goes wrong," Trixie said.

Kaela, Trixie and Angela, who were all wearing green,

crossed their fingers in front of their cameras.

Not one of them realised that green was extremely bad luck in the theatre.

Trixie stuck her foot in the stirrup and mounted, "I've just figured out something that we forgot to add to the agenda last night."

Angela looked up at her.

"Bart's last swim meet."

"When is it?"

Trixie shrugged, "Go find Bart's stalker, I'm sure she would be happy to find out."

Angela laughed and walked off in the general direction of Quiet Fire's stall to look for Kaela.

Trixie had a semi-private lesson with Wendy that day. She and Bella were the only two interested in dressage and so they were separated from the pack and taught to rule the ring. Trixie loved it.

Admittedly, she would love it more if Bella inexplicably lost all enthusiasm for dressage and went back to jumping.

"If only," Trixie said with a sigh.

The beginners were still being taught in the other ring when Trixie began warming Siren up. Her own class would not start for another twenty minutes, but she wanted to get as much practice as she could. Her very first competition with Siren was in three weeks. She needed to prove that her choice to buy Siren instead of a horse that was trained in dressage was for the best. Plus, it was about time Apley received dressage ribbons from someone other than the advanced riders.

"Looking good, Miss Beatrix."

Trixie smiled at the voice. She turned Siren around and nudged him over to the boy on the fence. Finley Bloom, relatively new at the stable, had taken an instant liking to Trixie. She had to admit that there were parts of him that fascinated her.

And then there was the rest of him that fascinated her more.

"How about this coming Saturday?" he asked.

"What about this Saturday?"

"Our night with the stars."

"Aren't you competing?"

"During the day."

"Yeah, but won't you be tired?"

Finley lifted one eyebrow, "Are you making excuses?"

"Not at all, I look forward to it."

"Good, me too. Now, tell me honestly. Would you like some help with the dressage?"

Everything in Trixie wanted to tell Finley to mind his own business, that she didn't need his help, that she could do it on her own.

But Finley had proven what a brilliant rider he was.

And if she wanted that blue ribbon, it would be in her best interest to listen.

At least about the dressage.

She could always ignore everything else.

Angela wandered over to Quiet Fire's stall, but couldn't find Kaela. Or Quiet Fire for that matter. Further down the corridor she could hear Bella on the phone, talking loudly about her new boyfriend. It was so typical of Bella to ignore the rules: mobiles and horses didn't mix. The exceptionally loud and annoying voice some people used when on their mobiles didn't mix with horses either. Angela rolled her eyes and wished she could beat some sense into Bella.

"Oh yeah, she's here. Why?" Bella said. "I don't care. I don't like her. She hangs out with the riff-raff anyway. Which is crazy because she is super-rich – she should be hanging out with the super-rich."

Angela rolled her eyes. Sometimes she wished she didn't need an excuse to beat Bella.

"I know. She purposely made friends with the poorest people at this stable. Maybe it's an ego thing. She hangs out with people who are lesser to her to make herself feel better. Who knows? I don't like her. And I think she paid those magazines to do those articles on her."

Suddenly Angela realised who Bella was talking about.

Bella was insulting Angela.

She blinked back tears and backtracked to the rings. She needed some friendly faces right now. Trixie was in the middle of a dressage lesson with Finley, and Kaela was nowhere to be seen. Jasmyn and Emily weren't at the stable yet, and Wendy was teaching. She refused to go back towards the stalls and risk encountering Bella. Instead she walked around the buildings and into the car park. She had to dodge Jeremy the donkey as he came trotting around the corner. She watched in horror as he trotted out the gate and turned left.

"You idiot! Get back here!"

She chased after him, but stopped dead when she saw that he had gone into old man Henry's property.

"There is no way I am going in there after you. I value my head too much."

He heehawed at her and turned his backside towards her.

"Oh you won't be so confident when he comes out of his house!"

"Who are you yelling at?"

Angela screamed in surprise and turned to face Kaela, "Where have you been?" she cried and threw herself into Kaela's arms.

"I had a meeting with the school newspaper. Why, what happened?"

Tears streamed down her cheeks, "Oh, just a verbal attack from Bella."

"What did she say?"

Angela repeated the conversation she had just heard.

"Riff-raff? I wasn't aware the most hated member of Apley was allowed to assign insults to the rest of us."

"Don't you care that she called you riff-raff?"

Kaela snorted, "I care more about the contents of the tissue every time I blow my nose."

"How can you not care?"

Kaela shrugged, "Wanna know what my dad tells me every time I get affected by something someone has said?"

"Yes."

"The wolf *does not* care about the opinion of the sheep."

Angela smiled, "Well, wolf, do you care about the opinion of the donkey?"

"Not particularly. Why?"

Angela turned and pointed towards Jeremy.

"Oh you idiot! Old man Henry is going to make a carpet out of you."

"So what are we going to do?"

Kaela pursed her lips and looked around.

"How about we go back to the stable and tell them we tried to get him out, but failed miserably? Then we can tell Wendy to send Bella to do the job."

Angela laughed, "That will sort my problems out."

Kaela linked her arm through Angela's and led her back to the stable, "You don't have a problem, you have a bully. And bullies only respond to strength. So be strong."

Angela nodded.

Be strong.

And don't care what the sheep thinks.

∽ Three ∾

"Operation 'punish Bella for making Angela cry' is about to commence."

Trixie nodded. Kaela climbed down from the fence, and walked towards the stalls. Trixie and Kaela were well-practised at punishing Bella. They managed to make her day as difficult as possible without even trying. Or even discussing it.

Kaela opened KaPoe's stall door and let herself in. The Thoroughbred stared at her in boredom. She reached under his saddle flap and loosened his girth.

"When she asks what happened," Kaela said to KaPoe, "You tell her that she should think twice before messing with the riff-raff."

Kaela quickly let herself out of the stall and raced over to Quiet Fire.

Who wasn't there.

"Why is he still in the field?" she asked her shadow.

The shadow ignored her.

"Kae," Wendy cried as the rider raced towards the field, "please ride Spirit. Quiet Fire isn't here, Moira has him at the beach for a photo shoot."

Kaela's shoulders slumped in disappointment, "Okay."

She quickly fetched Spirit's tack and got him ready for class. She noticed that she didn't have to adjust the stirrup leathers, which meant that no one else had ridden him. She sucked in her breath sharply. That thought was quite daunting. Did that mean that she was the sole trainer of the stable's only stallion?

Somewhere in the back of her head she remembered a news headline: *Mysterious Death of Felicity Willoughby Proves That Stallions Can Kill!*

She ignored it, the article was nonsense. Injuries had nothing to do with horses and everything to do with the riders.

"So why have they put your training in my hands?" she asked softly.

Spirit eyed her warily. Maybe he thought she was the wild and unpredictable one.

"Oi! You intermediates better get your behinds to the ring. I've got stuff to do."

Kaela smiled, Bart would be teaching the lesson.

Then she turned cold, Bart held nothing back in lessons. He made them earn the term 'rider'. Was Spirit up to the challenge?

Was she?

Once in the ring, she joined Russell, Emily and Jasmyn in warming up the horses. In the neighbouring ring, Bella led KaPoe over to the fence and mounted.

Or tried to.

The saddle slipped sideways under her weight and she fell to the ground and landed with a hard thump in a cloud of dust.

"Bella, the saddle goes on the back of the horse, not the side," Kaela called.

"And I don't know if you know this, but the girth has to be tight enough to support your weight," Trixie added, "or else you'll fall in the dirt."

Bella scowled at the both of them, got up, and adjusted KaPoe's saddle.

Bart ordered the jumpers to take their feet out of the stirrups and sit the trot. Kaela gritted her teeth against the pain. Spirit's trot was incredibly bouncy and she had to squeeze tighter with her calves than she ever had before. The pressure in her stomach muscles was grating.

"Are all four of you competing at Pignut Spinney?" Bart asked.

They all nodded.

"They have changed the rules. The intermediate jumps are going to be three-and-a-half feet high instead of three feet."

"Why did they do that?" Jasmyn asked.

Bart shrugged, "I don't know. I just work here."

"I'd fire you," Russell said.

"Oh come on, Russ," Bart said, "I'm sure no matter what height those jumps are your girlfriend will still beat you."

Everyone laughed.

"Or at least, it will *look* like she beat you."

Kaela looked over at Bart in shock. For weeks the Lost Kodas had assumed that Russell was letting his girlfriend win every competition, when he could easily have won. This was the first time someone besides the kodas had agreed with this assumption.

Unfortunately the quick jerk of Kaela's head startled Spirit, who shied sideways and almost ran Bart over. Because Kaela had no stirrups, she had to grab the pommel to stay on.

"Are you okay?" Bart asked as he grabbed Spirit's reins.

"Yes, I just forgot that it wasn't Quiet Fire I was riding."

Bart stroked Spirit's face and sighed, "Okay, we are going to have to tone the lesson down a smidge."

He sent Kaela back in line and told everyone to take up their stirrups. He then built a jump and had them practise this new height. Spirit refused every jump. By the time the lesson was over, Kaela wanted to bury her head in his mane and cry.

"Go gallop him," Bart said. "He has too much energy, he needs more riders."

Kaela turned Spirit and kicked him sharply. He raced for

the fence at a gallop, cleared it, and sped off towards the feeding paddock. He jumped that fence too. Kaela galloped him around the paddock twice, jumped him back over, raced him towards the ring, jumped him in and took the jump without a problem. It was only when she brought him to a stop that she realised that she had been crying the entire time.

Apparently, the wolf cares what the horse thinks.

"Don't worry, Bella. You got this. I'm sure you'll get it right next time," Trixie called.

Both Wendy and Bella looked at her in shock. She smiled sweetly at them. Wendy then gave them another complicated dressage move, which both girls managed easily.

"Oh well done, Bella," Trixie said, "I knew you had it in you."

Wendy gave the instruction for an even more complicated move. Trixie did it without a problem. Bella struggled through, and gave up.

"Next time, Bella, next time," Trixie said, "You can't push yourself too hard. You'll get it next time, I promise."

Wendy and Bella frowned at Trixie.

"Okay, Trix, you are up. Let's see a piaffe without stirrups."

Trixie did it without hesitation. Wendy seemed to be asking for everything Trixie had mastered weeks ago.

"Well done. Don't look so smug though. The judges will mark you down. Bella, you're up."

"Come on, Bella, I know you can do this," Trixie said.

All the 'encouragement' was starting to get under Bella's skin. She struggled to concentrate and get KaPoe under control. Her piaffe wouldn't even leave the starting gate.

"Oh too bad Bella, I really thought you had that one," Trixie said and shook her head, "Next time, I promise."

But Bella didn't get it the next time, or the time after, or even the time after that. And Trixie kept up her encouragement the entire way.

"Last move of the day, I want a canter without reins or stirrups, and you need to half-halt until you are at a complete stop. Trixie, you're first."

Trixie kicked her feet out of the stirrups and dropped her reins. She gripped tightly with her calves, sat firmly in the saddle, and nudged Siren into a canter. He started forward and moved into a slow canter. Trixie had trained him to only ever canter at a slow pace; it made everything that little bit easier. It was a trick she had learnt from Kaela's long-deceased mother. Beneath her, Siren cantered around the corner under guidance from her inside calf. She then released pressure slightly and rose up in her saddle. He slowed into a trot. She released more pressure and leaned back. He slowed to a walk. She released all pressure and sat as deeply into the saddle as she could. He came to a complete, and correct, halt.

Wendy clapped, then said, "Don't look so smug, they will dock points."

"Duly noted."

"Good, because I am not telling you again. Bella, your turn."

"Come on, Bella," Trixie cried, "You can do this. I know you can."

Bella scowled at Trixie and dropped her stirrups.

"Come on, Bella."

She nudged KaPoe, who sprang forward, jolting Bella and causing her free foot to knock his side. He dashed forward. Bella grabbed his mane to stay in the saddle. With her free hand she grabbed the reins and pulled him sideways. When she finally got control of him, she quickly put her feet back in the stirrups and put her hand up, to signal that she was resigning.

"You can do it next time, Bella," Wendy said with a shrug. "You are flustered and you're affecting KaPoe."

Bella sighed and nodded.

"Oh that's too bad, Bella. You were doing so well. But I know you'll get it next time. I have no doubts," Trixie said sweetly.

"Would you shut up?!" Bella screamed.

KaPoe, Siren, and the three horses in the jumping ring shied at her shrill voice.

"It's your fault I'm flustered!"

Trixie smiled sweetly, "My fault? Why, whatever do you mean?"

"All you have done for the whole lesson is bug me."

"Actually, she has been encouraging you all lesson," Wendy interrupted, "And you are showing some seriously unsportsmanlike conduct right now."

"She isn't being encouraging. She's trying to throw me off my game so she can wreck my chances of winning on Saturday."

"I would never," Trixie said with fake tears in her eyes.

"Oh well done, Bella, you've made Trixie cry," Russell said.

He was also well-practised in the art of punishing Bella.

"Bella, apologise to Trixie," Wendy said.

"For what?"

"For accusing her of sabotaging you, and then making her cry."

"I'm sorry," said Bella, without meaning it.

"That's better," Wendy said, "I will not have my riders accuse each other of imaginary crimes. Now all of you get on an outride and go home. Where is Kaela?"

Bart pointed to the galloping pair in the field. Wendy turned to look, sighed, and turned back to the riders, "What are you all still doing here?"

All jumpers and dressage riders were gone before that sentence fell from the air.

"Post for you."

Angela glanced over at the kitchen counter. Two envelopes with her name sat staring up at her.

"Who sends me mail?"

"I don't know, I can't see through envelopes."

Angela smiled at her mother, "Now there's a superpower."

"How was the stable?"

"Good," Angela said as she ripped the envelopes open. "Better than yesterday when Bella was gossiping about me. Today she wasn't even there. Although, Kaela was really struggling with Spirit. I think I need to help her."

"When are you lot going to the fair?" Gwendolyn asked.

"Not till next week. This Saturday is Trixie's big date, and we can't go without her."

"Ah, the big date with Dr Bloom's son, the science-hating one."

Angela nodded, she could relate.

"What do the letters say?"

"Both of them are from TV shows."

"Are they offering you a subscription?" Gwendolyn teased.

Angela shook her head, "They want to interview me."

Gwendolyn hurried over and read both letters.

"Do you watch these shows?"

Angela shook her head. They both raced for the lounge and turned the TV on. Eventually, they found one of the shows, *Sports Masters*. The presenters were at a cricket field

interviewing a girl who had just received her South African colours for wicketkeeping.

"Looks professional," Angela said.

The two then found the sister show, *Horse Masters*, on the internet. Both watched in wonder as international horse riders competed and were interviewed at various shows.

"I want to do it!" cried Angela as she spotted the third gold medal winner from the last Empire Games.

"Wait," Gwendolyn ordered, "TV is not an animal magazine."

"What do you mean?"

"I mean that you are leaving the safety of the *small* animal magazines and going onto TV, where you are open to any criticism from *anyone*. Are you sure that's what you want?"

All Angela could think about was Bella's voice saying, "I don't like her".

❦ Four ❧

"You will never guess what happened!"

Phoenix cried into the camera.

"What?" Trixie asked.

"My lead role broke her ankle."

"Is that part of the play?" Angela asked.

"No! The actress broke her ankle! She was climbing the ladder in high heels!"

"Who climbs a ladder in high heels?" Kaela asked.

"My former lead actress."

"That's terrible," Angela said.

"What are you going to do now? Trixie asked.

Phoenix shrugged, "We have an understudy. But she wasn't even my second choice"

"So why is she the understudy?" Kaela asked.

Phoenix's head snapped up and she glared at Kaela, "I will curse you!"

"Native Canadians don't believe in curses."

"I will invent one especially for you."

Kaela gulped. Phoenix could be quite intimidating when she wanted to be. It was the look of her, dark and ravishing – as though she commanded worlds with her fingertips.

"I'm sure that your understudy will be brilliant." Angela said.

"She had better be, or I'm going to force the other one onstage, crutches and all."

Wow, Kaela thought, never get on Phoenix's bad side.

"Everyone just keep your fingers crossed that nothing else goes wrong."

Phoenix had run her hands through her long hair, Kaela feared that she would start ripping large chunks out.

"My fingers are crossed for you," Angela said.

She lifted her hands to show the four pairs of crossed fingers. Her green bracelets glinted in the lamplight.

"Mine too," Trixie said and lifted her hands, "Even my hair is crossed," she grabbed her blonde plait to show Phoenix.

It was tied neatly with a green elastic.

"I'm crossing my toes," Kaela said and put her feet up on the desk.

"I don't want to see that," Phoenix said.

Kaela laughed and put her green socks back on.

The girls bade each other goodnight.

Kaela still had to write something for the school

newspaper, but she needed inspiration first. She got up and walked over to the bookshelves. She had organised with Tessigan, her editor, that she would write short stories instead of journalist articles. That way everyone was happy: Tessigan didn't have to threaten Kaela's life to get the article done, and Kaela was more than happy to write. Excitement bubbled up inside her at the thought of writing fiction. The world had opened up. She held a needleless compass and could go in any direction.

But what would she write about first?

Fantasy had always been her forte: the worlds of dragons, and the women who rode them. The kings and the queens they served. Centaurs and unicorns. A Pegasus and phoenix. That was her kingdom.

But what would she write?

Kaela had learned long ago that her brain had to find an idea, agree it was good and then send the message to her Muse. After a few days, the Muse would simply send the story in its entirety back to her brain. She never questioned it.

"An idea! An idea!" Kaela sang, looking around her father's study, "My kingdom for an idea."

She looked across the bookshelf. It was mainly filled with homeopathy books. Also battered textbooks and handled-to-tatters notebooks filled with her father's illegible scrawl from his years as a student in London. One shelf held huge hardback fiction books by an author named Anthony Henry. Her father loved his work.

Anthony Henry was a British author who had made his fame and fortune by writing historical dramas about South Africa. Her father had told her that one bleak, grey day in England during his first year of university, when he was lonely and miserable and hated his decision to study in another country, he had come across a picture of Bartholomew Diaz, the first European in South Africa, on a fiction book. The book had been called *The Naming of Natal*. He had grabbed it like a lifeline, knowing the myth of how Diaz had landed in South Africa on Christmas day and named the area Natal in honour of the day. That area was still named Natal, six hundred years later. Kaela's father didn't care that the book was parading the myth as fact, he devoured it any way. The book about his home town had made Leo Willoughby strong enough to face his life in a different country. Throughout his seven years at university, Anthony Henry had written a book a year. Interestingly enough, the publication of these books had coincided with Leo's darkest and saddest times.

Kaela had tried to read a few of his books. Tried being the optimum word. His books always reminded Kaela of an instruction manual. Historical fiction was not for her: by the time she had read half a page she felt as though she was in maths class. Although, Kaela begrudgingly had to admit, he obviously knew what he was doing. He was one of the most successful authors in the history of the world. His books earned so much money, he could support a small country for a century. There had been over thirty award-winning movies made from his work. He had launched the career of nearly every successful actor of the day. He had been on the bestseller list nearly every year for the last thirty years. He was synonymous with the dream of every aspiring writer the world over.

"Maybe I'll write to him and ask him his secret."

She laughed at that, he was probably living the high life in London and wouldn't answer the forty million fan mail letters he got a day.

"Maybe one day I will find the author who inspired him. Maybe their books will inspire me."

Maybe one day.

David Ren, the owner of the local Chinese restaurant, sauntered into Apley Towers that Thursday afternoon and had to be rescued by the riders.

David had made the colossal mistake of bringing food into the car park. Jeremy had him pinned to the wall before he had even registered the danger that lurked in the shadows.

"We are so sorry, Mr Ren," said Russell as he shooed Jeremy away.

"Would you like some tea?" Trixie asked, knowing that David had a habit of drinking English tea when stressed.

Much to the irritation of his Chinese family.

"No, I'm fine," he said with a wave of his trembling hand,

"I brought fortune cookies. They expire tomorrow, so I can't give them to customers."

"We'll give them a good home," Russell said excitedly.

David handed the brown paper bag over and hurried away.

"He'll never be back," Trixie said with a smile.

Russell dug in the paper bag and pulled out two cookies. He handed one to Trixie and opened the other.

"What does yours say?" Trixie asked.

Russell pulled it out and read it out loud, "What do you call a man with a paper bag on his head?"

"I don't know."

"Russell."

Trixie laughed and choked on her spit, "What are the odds?"

Russell didn't look very pleased, "How is that a fortune?"

Trixie recovered from her coughing fit and laughed even more, "How many fortune cookies are there in there? And you manage to pull out the one with your name on it? That is cosmic interference."

Russell rolled his eyes, "That thing belongs in a Christmas cracker, not a fortune cookie. What does your fortune say?"

Trixie held hers up to her face and read it quietly. Her eyebrows knotted above her nose.

"What's it say?"

"Hearts can only see the beauty of souls."

"What does that mean?" Russell asked.

"Oh you are such a boy. How can you not understand that?"

"Because a heart can't see. It has no eyes."

Trixie looked at him in exasperation, "Don't take it literally. Think about what it means in the figurative sense."

Russell sighed, closed his eyes and put his head back, "It means looks are superficial, not important and only your brain can see them. But your brain doesn't love, your heart loves. And your heart can only see souls."

Trixie smiled, "Why don't you use those smarts more often?"

Russell shrugged and pulled out another fortune cookie, "I do use them, you just choose not to see."

"I do see. I always see."

Russell laughed, put his hand on her shoulder and whispered, "You only ever see what you want to see."

Trixie stared into Russell's brown eyes; had they always been so bright and deep?

Had there always been that gold fleck in his left eye? Had his eyelashes always been so full and long?

"Ahem!"

Russell and Trixie turned to look at Elizabeth. He quickly pulled his arm away from Trixie and walked towards his girlfriend.

"Would you like a fortune cookie? They are either jokes or scarily profound."

Trixie left them and walked towards Siren.

At least she knew that she stood no chance of looking smug in the ring.

Not after that anyway.

⚜

"But wouldn't it be in your best interest to do these interviews?" Kaela asked.

Angela stopped grooming and looked over Dawn's back, "No," she simply said.

"Why not?"

"Because TV is dangerous."

"Can't possibly be more dangerous than riding."

Sometimes Angela wished that Kaela wasn't so daring, and was a little more understanding.

"I can't go on TV, I'll have the whole of South Africa mocking me."

"For riding well?"

"No ... for ... for ... well I don't know what for."

"So then what are you worried about?"

Angela sighed, why couldn't Kaela just be done with this topic?

"Do you need help with Spirit?" she asked to change the subject.

Kaela rolled her eyes, "I need a bodyguard."

"He's just young and spry."

"Well why does he have to be young and spry with me

41

on his back?"

"Because you have been trusted to train him."

Kaela pulled a face, "I have a writing course to apply for. And anyway, I have to go tack that demon horse."

"Gallop him first," Angela cried to the retreating rider.

Kaela put her hand up in answer but didn't turn around.

Angela finished grooming Dawn, gathered her equipment, and took it to the tack room.

Bart was in there, fiddling with his own locker. He was wearing chaps, which was odd as he was meant to be teaching the jumping class, not riding.

Angela threw her equipment in her locker and slammed the door shut before anything had a chance to fall out.

Bart laughed, "That seems safe."

"As long as I don't have to deal with it now."

"Don't do today what you can put off until tomorrow, huh?"

"That's my philosophy. Why are you wearing your chaps? Aren't you teaching?"

"I am teaching, but plans have changed slightly."

He shut his own locker and tapped his boot with a crop absentmindedly, "By the way, we need to get together sometime soon to practice for the Superius test. Are you sure you want to compete with Dawn? She is tiny."

"She can fly."

"She can fly eight-and-a-half feet can she?"

"Eight-and-a-half feet? Of course not!"

42

"Well that is how high those jumps get to."

Angela stared at him with big eyes. He stared back at her. With his green sweatshirt, his knee-high chaps and his dishevelled auburn hair, he reminded her of Peter Pan.

"Eight-and-a-half feet? Dawn isn't even that tall."

"Exactly. Use a different horse."

"Fergie doesn't jump."

Bart shook his head, "You are representing Apley. You can use any of the stable horses. Use Quiet Fire. No wait, he isn't a stable horse any more."

Before Angela could ask what he meant, he ploughed ahead.

"Use Toby. He is a brilliant jumper."

"He is a wimp, he won't jump eight-and-a-half feet."

Bart lifted his eyebrows, "Then use Spirit. He isn't a wimp. He is the only creature on earth who can bully Kaela. Which is saying something: even the mayor is scared of Kaela."

"Spirit is too much of a greenhorn. He can barely handle a lesson, how would he handle Equestrian International?"

Bart shrugged and tapped his crop against his ankle. Angela wished he was his best friend, Björn. She missed him. She missed his rust-coloured hair and shy smile.

She sighed and changed the subject, "When is you last swim meet?"

Bart paled visibly, "In four weeks."

"And then what happens?"

"If I place anywhere, I get to represent South Africa in

43

the Empire Games." He looked at his watch, "Gotta go, Ang. The intermediate class is starting."

She nodded.

"And I need you to teach it."

Kaela mounted Spirit.

She sent a silent wish to the cosmos to make this lesson go well. She nudged the stallion and led him to the rings. Bart, mounted on his horse Mouse, stood waiting just outside the advanced ring.

"Are you teaching from the saddle today?"

"Yep. I was thinking about that horse, and I know what he needs."

"What?"

Bart gestured with his head. "Follow me," he gathered his reins and nudged Mouse.

"What about the lesson? Who's going to teach?"

Kaela looked into the ring where Angela stood waiting for the rest of the riders.

"Have fun," she said with a smile.

"Are you coming?" Bart called.

Kaela nudged Spirit and quickly caught up with Mouse.

"So what's his problem?"

Bart looked over at Spirit, "He gets too excited."

Kaela shrugged, "He's young."

"Exactly. And what do young people love to do?"

"I don't know, what?"

"Play."

Bart led her to the feeding paddock, leaned down and opened the gate. Kaela led Spirit through and looked at the giant beach ball in the field.

"What are we playing?"

"Apley Knock'ems."

Kaela laughed, "Can Spirit play that?"

"All horses can."

Apley Knock'ems was a game Wendy had invented when she had first started the riding school. It was like football crossed with polo: two mounted riders stood on either end of a 'court' and used the horse to kick the giant ball back and forth. The first horse and rider team to miss a kick lost.

"You go on that side," Bart pointed, "I'll get the ball moving."

He nudged Mouse into a canter towards the ball, and the bay gelding kicked the toy towards Spirit. Kaela squeezed her calves and turned him; he cantered towards it but missed.

"I win."

Kaela nodded and led Spirit over to the ball. She kept him at a walk while he kicked the toy back to the court area.

"You put it into motion."

Bart nodded and nudged Mouse forward. The ball came back towards Kaela. This time Spirit understood, he responded more quickly and kicked the ball back. Mouse

knocked it back towards him without a hitch. Spirit didn't bother waiting for a command, he raced forward and kicked the ball like the world championship depended on it.

Bart, being lazy, was letting Mouse do all the work, and took too long to react. The ball flew past them, leaving them both to stare after it.

"Woohoo! Well done, Spirit!" Kaela cried and wrapped her arms around his neck.

He brought his nose around and rubbed it against her toes.

"Okay, last game," Bart said as Mouse kicked the ball back, "Then we're going to do something else."

Mouse put the ball into play, Spirit kicked it back. Mouse knocked it again, Spirit bolted and sent it back. Kaela was having so much fun that she forgot how much of a difficult ride Spirit was. Her calves gripped Spirit's side without pain. She had found just the right amount of pressure to keep him responsive and keep her safe.

She had also discovered that once Spirit understood what was expected of him, this slightest touch of the reins brought the desired task. This was new to Kaela. Spirit had been born and trained at a stud farm that used very gentle methods to teach their horses. He was obviously not used to the way Kaela demanded things. In her defence, she had spent the majority of the last few years riding only one horse – a very stubborn horse who needed constant reminders that he was not in charge.

Suddenly, she realised that it was her that was in the

wrong, not Spirit.

"It's me!" she cried, and missed the ball.

Spirit stared after it sadly.

"It's you what?" Bart asked.

"It's me that's messing things up with Spirit."

Bart nudged Mouse over, "Meaning?"

"Quiet Fire is stubborn and I have to fight him, so I think I have to fight Spirit as well. But I don't."

She dropped the reins, moved her right leg forward and squeezed with her calf. Spirit turned right. Bart smiled his gorgeous half-smile.

"Could you do that with Quiet Fire?"

"Nope."

"This is why they tell you to ride different horses."

"I finally understand," Kaela exclaimed.

"Come on, let's do another exercise."

Bart made her walk the paddock and look for natural obstacles. She insisted on doing this without reins. Spirit seemed to be enjoying himself as he dipped the hills and climbed the banks. She turned him using pressure from her calves and halted him by leaning back.

Bart watched this with a smile, "He'd respond well to dressage training."

Kaela scowled at him, "What wasted talent. He was obviously born to jump and race, why make him do ballet?"

Bart lifted one eyebrow, "Black Satin did both."

Kaela's heart froze at the mention of her mother's stallion.

"But I suppose Black Satin was one of a kind. There have been very few to match him."

Kaela nodded curtly.

"I don't think I have ever seen a horse that can go from the dressage ring to the cross country circuit so easily."

"Could go."

"Pardon?"

"He could go from the dressage ring to cross country. He doesn't any more, and hasn't for many years."

Bart nodded, "How old is he now?"

Kaela did a quick calculation in her head, "Seventeen."

"He would be retiring soon. You know … If your mum …"

"I know. But he is happy on the farm."

"I wonder if he misses the glory?" Bart mused.

Kaela just wondered if he missed Felicity.

❧ Five ❧

Trixie nervously pushed the heavy wooden doors open. The planetarium was dark. Her heart gave a little skip when she saw Finley at the top of the stairs.

"Come this way, fair lady."

He gestured to her, and she slowly climbed the stairs. She wanted to turn around and go home. She wasn't ready for a relationship with Finley. She wished this wasn't a date. There was a pressure on the evening that she was not in the mood to deal with. Her eyes could see his soul and it was perfect, but for some reason her heart wouldn't get on board.

"Hi, Miss Science," Finley said with a smile, "are you ready for a night with the stars?"

Trixie forced a smile, "Yes."

The two went into the domed room and took their seats.

"Neck ache commencing," Finley said.

"Where is your dad?"

"Behind the scenes. He needs his textbooks: I warned him about you."

Trixie laughed and then jumped as the lights turned off and the dome's ceiling erupted into galaxies.

"Hello Trixie," a voice came through a speaker in the armrest.

"Hello Dr Bloom," she answered, "how are you?"

"I'm very well, thank you. Would you be okay with me starting off with the same show we do for the kids? You can jump in any time with any questions, and we'll just go from there."

"Sounds perfect," she said excitedly.

"Brilliant," Dr Bloom said and began the tour through the solar system.

Two hours later, Dr Bloom admitted that he hadn't worked that hard at finding an answer or been so terrified of a question since he had written his PhD thesis on the Higgs boson.

"You definitely know your stuff, Miss King. I strongly suggest a career in astrophysics," Dr Bloom said as he sat down next to his son.

Trixie wrinkled her nose, "I'm still trying to figure out what direction to head in. I mean, I love astrophysics –"

"Obviously," Finley interrupted.

"But I don't think I'm cut out for running a planetarium or teaching. I have very little patience for humans."

"I love how she says that as though she isn't one," Finley said to his father.

"So what would you prefer to do?" Dr Bloom asked.

Trixie gave a mischievous glance to Finley, "Lately I have really enjoyed trying to invent things."

"I got that started," Finley said with pride.

"Well, we do need scientists to design and build space shuttles and interplanetary probes. Especially now that we are moving away from fossil fuels. Do yourself a favour, Trix, start learning about alternative energies now so that one day when you are designing Apollo Thirty or the next Voyager, you can use an energy that space programs will be willing to back. Get ahead of the game."

"Good advice, Dad."

Dr Bloom looked sideways at his son, "You were listening? Since when do you listen to science?"

"I found your tour through the galaxy quite fascinating."

Trixie lifted her eyebrows.

"Just our galaxy?" Dr Bloom asked, "Did my tour go through only our galaxy?"

"Ah … yes?"

"Wrong. We also went into Andromeda."

"He was asleep by that point," said Trixie.

"I'm not surprised," Dr Bloom said with a wave of his hand.

"You can't blame me. When I was a kid you used to read me to sleep. Now when you are talking and it's dark, of course I'm going to fall asleep."

Dr Bloom rolled his eyes and got up, "I have to go sort the office out. Goodbye, Trixie. It was lovely to meet you."

Trixie shook his hand and watched him walk off.

"Did you have fun?" Finley asked as he rubbed his eyes.

"Did you?"

"Immensely. I dreamt I won a pig-raising competition."

"Weird."

"On Jupiter."

"Impossible."

"In winter."

"Although the planet spins on its axis, it does not have an atmosphere. Therefore there is no winter as we recognise it."

Finley leaned back and pretended to snore. She flicked his shoulder.

"I like you better when you're talking about horses," he said.

"Well good thing I never get bored of that topic," Trixie replied. "Now, tell me again how Angela beat you in the dressage today."

"Seriously now, do you go into the show ring and just expect to win?"

"Of course not."

Björn put his hands up, "So why do you keep winning?"

"Because I work hard."

"That's your secret, I think. You don't think about winning, so you win."

"I win because I work my brains out," Angela snapped.

Björn raised his eyebrows, "Okay, sorry I mentioned your success. Who else won?"

"Finley came second. Warren came third."

"Who's Warren?"

"Another Apley rider."

"So Apley cleaned house?"

Angela nodded, "If only we could dominate in jumping as well."

"Maybe I should ride," Björn said and cracked his fingers, "I'll show you all how it is done."

Angela didn't laugh, she didn't even smile.

"Ooookay, how about I don't say anything?"

Angela didn't respond, she looked around David's Chinese Restaurant. On Saturday night it was always full of couples. Admittedly, they were all far happier than Angela and Björn were at that moment. At least they were talking. Angela closed her eyes and sighed. She was tired, not just from her earlier competition, but from the entire Season. They were only halfway through, and she already wished she could go to sleep and wake up when it was over.

She opened her eyes and looked at Björn. He stared out of the big glass windows into the chilly night.

"What are you thinking about?"

Slowly, his gaze crossed over to hers, "I'm imagining what it would be like if our winters were like northern hemisphere winters."

"What do you mean?"

"Well, look into the night. Imagine huge, fluffy, white snowflakes coming down."

"I've never seen snow," Angela admitted.

"It's great – cold and wet – but great. Look into the night and imagine snowflakes coming down."

Angela turned to look into the car park. She tried to see falling flakes but couldn't.

She shook her head, "I can't."

Björn pushed the chair back and came around the table, he sat down on the empty chair next to her. She twisted around in her own chair so that she faced him. He put one hand on her knee and used the other to point outside.

"See the street light? Imagine that in the triangle of light there are fat pieces of white fluff. They see-saw down to the ground. As soon as they touch anything they melt. The colder it becomes, the more flakes fall. Soon there is a light covering of powder on the floor. Can you see it?"

Angela smiled and nodded, "What happens if it lands on your skin?"

"It melts as soon as it hits you. And then you are left with a splodge on your face."

"How cold is it?"

"Cold! You know when you open the freezer and get a face full of icy wind? It feels like that all the time. Your toes are permanently frozen."

Angela laughed, "So in a perfect world, you would have a snowy winter?"

Björn nodded, "I would, yes."

Angela thought she would like to see snow, but she wasn't so sure she could handle that cold and it would probably make riding difficult.

"What's your perfect world?" Björn asked.

"Appearing on those TV shows so that someone besides my father knows how hard I work on a horse."

Björn nodded and leaned forward. "So do the interviews," he whispered into her ear.

"It's too risky."

"How so?"

Angela frowned, she didn't know what bugged her more: that question, or the fact that she had no answer to it.

Björn leaned back against the wall, "You need tougher skin for this business."

"What if people see me and mock me?"

Björn shrugged, "Ignore them."

"Easier said than done."

Björn sighed and scratched his chin, "Want some advice from the kid who was always bullied and always the last to be picked for anything?"

Angela nodded.

"If people insult you and what they say is not true, then laugh. If what they say is true, then change it."

"I'm not that brave."

He grabbed her hands, "For your dreams you need to be."

"Kaela, get dressed into decent people's clothes. We are going out."

She sighed and walked into her father's study, where he was quickly scribbling from a battered textbook.

"Can't you go without me?"

"No, I'm not leaving you home alone."

Kaela looked around the dark house, "Where's Gramoo?"

Leo shrugged, "I think the woman has a boyfriend she isn't telling us about."

"Why can't I just stay? I don't feel like restaurant food and making small talk."

"We are not going to a restaurant. We're going to the home of one of my patients in order to teach his mother how to cook the food he needs in the next month."

Kaela's eyes widened, "So what am I supposed to do?"

Leo sighed, "I don't know. Go swimming with Bart, or go harass the horses, or get into that giant cage with the turtle. I don't care what you do, just stay out of my hair while I teach Wendy."

"We're going to Apley?"

"Not with you dressed like that. Pyjamas with skiing polar bears on them may have been cute when you were four, but at fourteen it makes me an unfit father."

Kaela raced up the stairs and threw on some clothes and shoes. She ran a brush through her hair, or tried to.

Eventually she gave up and grabbed her hair clip, piled the hair on top of her head, and pinned it down.

"Now stay that way," she ordered the mess.

One stray strand fell from the clip and sat between her eyes. She sighed and tucked it behind her ear.

"Why does my hair never behave when I need it to?"

"Are you coming any time before my retirement?" Leo cried. "I've aged a century down here."

Kaela raced down and out the front door.

"Wrong way," Leo cried, "We're taking the car."

She backtracked through the house and into the garage, "Why are we driving there? You know it's just down the road right?"

Leo opened the boot displaying large grocery bags of food, four pots, a bamboo steamer and a blender, "You want to carry all that?"

"No," Kaela said and hopped into the front seat. "Did I tell you that I've been riding a new horse?"

"You mean you weren't superglued to Quiet Fire?" Leo asked as he started the engine and buckled up.

"Apparently not. And I found out why they tell you to ride many different horses. Although, by this age I fully believed I would have my own horse."

"By this age, I used to believe my practice would be ten times its size and I would have three other children who would be supported by my wife's International Sporting Championship winnings, while I paid the mortgage on the enormous house we would need."

"International Sporting Championship winnings wouldn't support a family of six."

Leo laughed, "We lived really well off of her winnings before you were born. The Empire Games cheque paid for a Baltic cruise with a two week holiday in Russia."

"Yes, but the International Sporting Championships are only every four years."

"But the Empire Games is every year. And she won every year. We bought our first house off two years of winnings."

"But if she had four kids, that would mean she was pregnant for thirty-six months. That's at least four Empire Games she would have had to stay out of."

Leo nodded as he pulled up into Apley's car park, "Good point. After you were born she stopped competing anyway."

"Why?"

"Because you never slept. We were both so sleep-deprived I once made her a banana smoothie using only the peels instead of the actual bananas. And neither one of us noticed until we had a troop of monkeys congregating around the discarded bananas. Which, by the way, I had put back into the fruit bowl for some unknown reason."

Kaela laughed as she got out of the car.

Leo opened the boot and handed her the pots, "It would have been too dangerous for her to compete in that state. Which just shows that you need to get everything done before you have kids. Because once those kids come, there are no more Baltic cruises or balloon rides over the

Drakensburg Mountains. There are only sleepless nights and banana skin smoothies."

Kaela followed Leo up the stairs to Wendy's front door, "You make me sound like a burden."

"Not at all. Did you not just hear me say I wanted three more of you?"

"You wanted four girls?"

Leo nodded as he rang Wendy's doorbell, "I always believed it was my lot in life to be surrounded by amazing women."

"So you have a girlfriend now, have three more daughters."

"Oh no, thank you. The thought of having to start all the way from the beginning again makes me want to cry. I can finally go on Baltic cruises again, why ruin it?"

"So why don't we ever go?"

"Are you going to pay for it?" Leo asked as Wendy opened the door.

"No, I'm not paying, we have a deal," Wendy said as she wrapped her arms around Leo and kissed him on the nose.

Wendy was the only one on earth who was allowed to kiss Leo's nose. Not even Kaela could do it. Their friendship ran deep.

"What deal do you have?" Kaela asked as she followed Leo to the kitchen.

"You are riding for free," he said as he began unpacking the grocery bags.

"Really?"

"Yes," Wendy said as she got mugs out and put the kettle on, "what's the point of the money going back and forth?"

"Although you owe me dinner for this dinner," Leo said, and gestured to all the food.

Wendy smiled and nodded. "Bart's by the pool," she said to Kaela.

"I'll let you know when dinner is ready," Leo said.

Kaela nodded. As she left the room, she heard her father say: "The older she gets, the more questions she has about Felicity. I'm going to need something a little stronger than tea after that last conversation."

Kaela found Bart on the swing in the pool area. He had an almost-empty bottle of water in the one hand, and his mobile in the other. She went over and sat on the other swing. A few years ago, the Willoughbys had had dinner with the Oberons every second week. Then both families had gotten busy and drifted apart. Kaela wondered how different things would have been if dinner with the Oberons had still been a fixture on the Willoughbys' calendar. But then she wondered what life would have been like if Felicity had given up riding altogether and stayed home that day instead of disappearing. Would Kaela now have three sisters? Would she know Bart and Wendy? Would she know Trixie and Angela?

"Do you ever wish your mom had other children?"

"No," Bart said as he put his mobile away and sipped the last of his water, "I like being the only child. I struggle to share my mother with other riders."

"My dad said that he wanted three more daughters."

"So?"

"So, he has Niamh now, what if he turns around and does have three more? I don't want to share my dad."

Bart laughed, "It's like they are our toys and no one but us can play with them."

"That is exactly how I feel."

"I suppose, at the end of the day, it isn't our choice."

Kaela sighed and looked up at the sky, the full moon shone down on them, lighting the night and filling her mind with thoughts of fairy tales in ancient forests.

"I've been thinking about Spirit," Bart said.

"What about him?"

"He is a Kladruber."

"Well done, Sherlock. How long did it take you to figure that out?"

Bart smiled and looked over at Kaela, "Just hear me out. Spirit is a black Kladruber. A very rare breed in an even rarer colour," Bart took a deep breath, "And, well ... Black Satin was a Kladruber as well. And he is –"

"Black," Kaela interrupted.

"Exactly. Two very rare horses, in an even rarer colour, and both seem to be good at both dressage and jumping."

"So what's your point?"

"Don't you find that odd? I mean, what are the chances?"

Kaela shrugged.

"I've been trying to research on my mobile if they are related, but I don't know what the stud farm called Spirit before we bought him."

"Stallion number twenty-seven," Kaela said as she remembered what the owner had told her the day he'd dropped him off.

Bart nodded, "Thanks, that will make the search easier."

They both looked up at the moon.

"I love the full moon. It makes me wish I was a wolf and I could howl at it."

"I wouldn't put it past you," Bart said.

Kaela smiled, cupped her hands around her mouth, and howled. Bart laughed and joined in. The three stable dogs raced into the pool area and howled along with them. Eventually the humans gave up; the dogs were putting them to shame.

"I wish I could bottle moonlight. I'd put it up on my shelf and forevermore have the full moon in my room," Kaela sighed, her eyes clouded over with visions of the impossible.

Bart grabbed his empty bottle, stood up and walked to the pool.

"What are you doing?"

Kaela watched as Bart walked to the shimmering patch of water that reflected the moon. He dipped the bottle into the reflection and filled it up. Then, he screwed on the lid and brought it over to Kaela. He knelt in front of her swing and handed the bottle over.

"Bottled moonlight."

She smiled and took it, "Thank you."

He grabbed her calves and pulled her forward, "I'll make you a deal. You help me research the ancestors of both horses and then I'll drop it. But I need your help."

Kaela looked at her bottled moonlight, "I don't want to see any articles on Black Satin."

Bart nodded and stood up.

With one more glance towards the moon, Kaela got up off the swing.

Five minutes later they were in Bart's room. Kaela sat on the loveseat at his bay window and stared at the stables while Bart searched the internet on his computer.

"Okay, thanks to you I've found the list of Black Satin's ancestors. Now I just have to find Spirit's."

Kaela could see a few horses in the fields. Spirit was there too, although she could only see the white star on his face. The rest of him blended in with the night.

"Stallion number twenty-seven. Click. Waiting for the link to load. It's loaded. Comparing the two …"

"Do you always narrate your actions?"

"No one else to do it for me."

"Is it nice to be able to see the riding rings from your room?"

"It's nice to watch the intermediate classes while I'm doing my homework."

Kaela turned away from the window and looked around

the room. The last time Kaela had been in Bart's room, he'd had a bedspread with cartoon characters on it. Now he had a simple blue and white design. Where there used to be posters of the same cartoons, now there were swimming certificates and an Oberon coat of arms.

Kaela stared in wonder at a clock with a wolf and full moon on it.

Sometime in the last few years, Bart had grown up. He was no longer the young little thing that had first caught her attention. She looked down at her bottled moonlight. Something inside her knew that if she had met Bart for the first time only five minutes ago, she would still feel the same way about him.

There was something about him that called to her.

"I like your Buddha."

Bart looked across at the wooden Buddha statue, "Thank you. So do I."

He leaned over and rubbed the stomach for luck.

Kaela got up and went to the bookshelf; all the books were new too. Kaela was quite surprised to see *The Naming of Natal* by Anthony Henry. It didn't exactly seem like Bart's type.

"Oh my word," Bart said and sat up straight. "They are both descendants of the same horse."

"What?" Kaela cried and rushed over.

"Time Traveller. He's on both lists."

"But these lists aren't all the ancestors."

66

"No, just the ancestors that have achieved something. Look, the list stops at his name both times, which means he was the first in the lineage to do something."

"What did he do?"

"I don't know. But we're gonna find out."

Bart quickly typed the horse's name into the search engine. Over two thousand articles came up.

"Wow, who was this horse?"

He clicked on the first link and waited for it to load. The screen was suddenly filled with an old black and white newspaper photo of a horse who was a twin of both Black Satin and Spirit. The headline beneath him said: Time Traveller Takes Double Gold in 1956 Empire Games.

"Double gold?" Kaela asked.

Bart quickly scanned the article, "Time Traveller became the first horse to win gold in both dressage and jumping."

He quickly went back to the search engine and found a different article.

"Time Traveller made history in 1956, and again in 1960, by becoming the first horse to take gold in both dressage and show jumping competitions. A feat that would not be repeated again until Felicity Willoughby, riding Black Satin, won double gold forty years later."

"It didn't mention that Black Satin was a descendant," Kaela said.

"Look when this article was written. They didn't have easy access to internet information yet. They didn't know."

"And Spirit? The stud farm didn't say a thing about him."

"But Time Traveller is listed on their website. They obviously didn't know how important Time Traveller was."

"So the youngest descendant of the world's first double winner is standing in the feeding paddock as we speak? And is showing all the same signs as both his famous cousin and his more famous great-grandfather?"

Kaela and Bart looked out into Apley where Spirit's white star stared back at them.

Almost as though he knew what they had just discovered.

❧ Six ❧

Phoenix: You will never guess what just happened.

Angela: Oh no! What?

Phoenix: Our lead male got food poisoning.

Trixie: What was he eating?

Phoenix: I don't know!

Kaela: Find out so you don't eat it.

Phoenix: This is a nightmare! What else could go wrong?

Kaela: DON'T SAY THAT!

Trixie: THAT IS JINXING YOURSELF!!!!!!!!!!

Angela: Quick! Say, 'Nothing else can go wrong!'

Phoenix: NOTHING ELSE CAN GO WRONG!!!!!

Angela quickly shut off the computer and walked the length of the house to make sure she was home alone. She raced back to the study, pulled a piece of paper from her back pocket, and dialled the first number.

"Hello," a haughty voice answered.

"Hi, my name is Angela May. I'm just –"

"Of course, Miss May. We have been looking forward to your call. Have you decided to appear on our show?"

Angela took a deep breath and said with a shaky voice, "Yes, I have."

"Oh that's excellent. Let me just see now," Angela could hear pages being turned. "Ah, I see you are entered into the Superius test on Saturday. Equestrian International has invited us to come and film it. How would you feel about doing the interview either before or after the test?"

Deep breath, "I would love to."

"Okay then, Miss May. I'm scheduling you in. Just look out for us on the day. We will be displaying our show's name on our clothes."

Angela thanked her and bade her goodbye. She replaced the phone and said, "One down, one to go."

She dialled the next number. This time a male answered.

"*Sport Masters*, Gary speaking."

"Hello there, my name is Angela May."

"Angela!" he cried, "We thought we would never hear from you. We were hoping to interview you at Apley riding school before the end of the month. What do you think?"

"Uhm … Sure, that works for me."

She was only slightly surprised by how on the ball these people were. Maybe she wasn't entering the shark tank after all.

"Okay, when I have more details I'll call. Can I call you on this number?"

"Uhm, no. Use my mobile number."

She gave him the number and waited while he scribbled it down.

"One last thing, Angela," he said, "Don't say 'uhm' – be confident! You are a master of your own destiny, and masters don't say 'uhm'."

"Thanks for the advice. I look forward to your call."

She bade him goodbye and put the phone down. She stood in the empty study, her heart pounding loud enough to attract Martians. Before she knew what she was doing she'd dialled a number and was waiting with barely concealed impatience while the phone rang in her ear.

"Hello," said a male voice.

"I did it!" she cried.

"You did what?" Björn asked.

"I called the TV shows and organised to be interviewed."

Björn was quiet for a second, "You mean to tell me that I have a famous girlfriend? I'm going to tell everyone."

"No, don't. I did it without my parents' permission."

Björn was quiet again, "Ahh, my girlfriend – the rebel."

Angela smiled and lifted one eyebrow, "Wanna meet somewhere and you can show me the snow?"

Five minutes later Björn rode up to the gate on his motorbike, "So where are we going?"

"I'm not going with you on that."

"Oh, you'll ride a horse but not a motorbike?"

"Horses are safer."

"I doubt that."

Björn handed her his spare leathers and helmet, there was a part of her that had always wanted to try these things on. She slowly took them and put them on.

"How do I look?"

"Fabulous. Now get on."

Angela gulped, took a deep breath, got on, and wrapped her arms around his waist. She watched as he used his foot to put it into gear and his hands to accelerate.

Not all that different from a horse, she thought.

She kept her eyes closed and a tight grip on Björn the entire ride. Once there, he turned the motorbike off and put the stand up.

"There, now I have ridden your horse and you have ridden mine. You can let go now. You're cutting off my blood flow.

Ang! Ang! Put your feet on the ground."

Slowly she let go and got off.

"There is no way that was scarier than riding a horse," Björn said.

"It was. I saw my life flash before my eyes."

"Was it any good?"

Angela smiled, "An award-winner."

Björn took her for a drink on the promenade. They sat at the very last table and watched the ocean crash against the lighthouse.

"Why aren't you at the stable?"

Angela shrugged, "Avoiding Bella."

"That rich jerk with the fake British accent?"

Angela laughed, Björn was the first person to notice Bella's fake speech. Angela had been starting to believe she was imagining it.

"Yes, her."

"Why?"

She quickly told Björn about the conversation she had heard.

"I don't understand why you have to avoid her."

"Because she hurt me."

"Do you like her?" he asked.

"No."

"Then what does it matter if she doesn't like you? Technically that works out for the best."

Angela shrugged and looked back at the sea. Björn leaned

down to scratch his ankle. He hit his head on the table and looked at Angela in shock when she laughed.

"I feel the support."

Angela's smile fell from her face, "Well that's it, I thought Apley Towers was going to be so different."

"How so?"

"My last stable was so horrible. The people were absolute creeps. Especially this one girl, Gemma. They were all so mean. Especially her. And whenever I beat her at anything, she was even worse."

"Apley is different. There is one girl who is a jerk, and trust me, people put her in her place. Apley is full of great people who will support you no matter what … even if you hit your head on the table."

"My laughter is my support."

Björn fake scowled.

"I have to practise jumping with Bart sometime this week."

Björn frowned, "And?"

"And you are expected to be there to stop me from killing him."

"Why are you going to kill my friend?"

"Because he dares to think he knows more about jumping than I do."

"He said that about you the other day … I'm joking, by the way."

"Maybe someone needs to be around to stop me from killing you."

"Who is going to stop your parents from killing you when they find out what you've done?"

Angela put her face in her hands, "I'll have to break it to them slowly."

"Make them dinner, then clean the kitchen."

Angela's eyebrows lifted, "That's not a bad idea."

"I'm well trained in breaking bad news to parents. I get up to mischief at least twice a week. In fact, I'm cooking dinner for my father tonight."

"Kaela, Kaela."

Two beginners ran up with huge eyes and tear-stained cheeks.

"What happened?"

"We were playing cricket, and I hit the ball too hard," Shanaeda said with a trembling lip.

"I wasn't aware you could hit the ball too hard."

Both girls nodded, "It went over the wall and broke old man Henry's window," Amy cried with fresh sobs.

Kaela's stomach dropped into her pelvis. She looked towards the next house in fear.

"Oh Shakespeare's quill!" Kaela cried when she found her voice.

"We didn't mean it," Shanaeda sobbed and threw herself into Kaela's waist.

She wrapped her arms around her and squeezed tightly. Amy did the same.

Soon Kaela's air supply began to run dangerously low.

"Okay, okay. Let go. I'll go over and apologise and see what happens. Go tell Wendy what happened."

"She isn't here. That's why class was cancelled."

"Where is she?"

Both girls shrugged.

"Go find Derrick and tell him. Make sure everyone knows where I am. That man might keep me for his vampire ceremonies."

The girls nodded and ran off. Kaela breathed deeply. If this is what happened when class was cancelled, she would personally make sure class was never cancelled again.

She walked out of Apley's car park, turning to take one last look at the gate with its wrought-iron horse welded onto it. She slowly walked into old man Henry's front garden. Her heart beat in her ears. Her fingers were sweating into her closed fists. He had a wooden porch which went around the entire house. Two rocking chairs sat on either side of the front door while a large swing hung suspended from the ceiling, speaking of a time when old man Henry might have been a nice person who entertained company and regaled them with stories of South Africa over the last century.

Or maybe the one before that, he looked old enough.

She climbed the front steps with ice in her veins, and slowly crept across the porch. There was a gold knocker on the door, interestingly enough, in the shape of a horseshoe. She grabbed it and banged it loudly.

"Who's there?"

As always, Kaela was surprised by the pristine English accent. His face did not suit it. The accent made him seem like an aristocrat who had run away from the green hills of England and spent the rest of his life brooding in the harsh South African sun.

"Hello Mr Henry. My name is Kaela Willoughby. I'm from the riding school. I came to apologise for the window."

The door yanked open, Kaela stepped back in shock.

"Do modern children have no respect for anything?"

"I'm sure ancient children caused just as much havoc."

"Are you suggesting I am ancient?"

Kaela quickly shook her head.

"Come in and wait while I write to that woman next door."

"Her name is Wendy Oberon," Kaela said fiercely.

Old man Henry raised his eyebrows in amusement, "I'll be sure to mention her rude messengers."

"Well you can only take the moral high ground if you are not rude. And calling your neighbour 'that woman' is very derogatory."

"My, my … She has big words."

"My words are prodigious."

For a split second, old man Henry looked surprised.

"Come, we are wasting time. Close the door behind you, you are letting the cold in."

Kaela stepped into the house, took one last look at daylight, and shut the door.

"Aren't you from England? How can you think this is cold?"

"Because cold is cold: it doesn't matter that there are different variations of the phenomenon, I am still cold."

"Do you miss the snow?"

"If I missed the snow, I would live where it snowed."

"What part of England are you from?"

"Do you ever hold your tongue?"

"No, my hands are usually full of horse germs, holding my tongue would be diabolical for my health."

Old man Henry laughed but didn't answer her. He was bent over a table scribbling rapidly.

Kaela looked around. His house looked like a library whose caretakers had fled the scene decades ago. Books lined every wall and sat on every surface. It was Kaela's dream home.

Minus the dust.

She went to examine the books. They were mostly Victorian. There were very few from Kaela's lifetime or even the lifetime of her parents. Secretly she was pleased: even more proof that old man Henry was a vampire, born around two centuries ago. She ran her hands over the cracking leather spines. And inhaled the scent of her childhood.

"*Frankenstein*," she whispered as she spotted the black book.

She took it down and slowly opened the cover.

To Ianthe,
For I shall be happy if anything I ever produce may exalt
and soften sorrow, as the writings of the divinities of our race
have mine.
Ever affectionately yours,
Mary

Her heart stopped beating, the old man next door had a signed copy of Frankenstein? It must be worth more than her father's house. She quickly put it back. She looked through the rest of the books, she knew them by reputation but had never attempted them. All Victorian authors, their names in faded gold ink on black cracking covers. On a whim she took down *A Christmas Carol* and opened it.

To Nelly – my magic circle of one.
Love,
Charlie

Kaela's breath caught in her throat. A signed copy. She put it back quickly.

Old man Henry had disappeared from the room. She didn't know what was worse: having him near, or not knowing where he was. She turned back to the books and stopped in her tracks.

Alice's Adventures in Wonderland.
She picked it up with trembling hands and opened it.

To my darling,
You make me wonder if the snow loves the trees and fields.
All my love, in secrecy,
your Cheshire Cat

Kaela nearly fainted when she saw the signature under the pet name. The man who had signed it was the man who had written the book. Unwillingly, she put it back. She didn't recognise the rest of the books, but soon the open shelves gave way to glass cases. The books inside looked as though they would fall apart in a stiff breeze. She couldn't be certain because the words had faded, but she could have sworn the one book was written by a Henry R. She knew enough about history to know that the R meant royalty, and that the only King Henry who wrote books was Henry the Eighth, who had reigned over four hundred years before. An old man in South Africa couldn't possible possess a book that should be in a museum. Could he?

He came back into the room and resumed writing. She tried to ignore him. He did the same.

She moved past the shelves and into the lounge. Books were stacked up and used as tables, which surprised her. They were modern, with dust jackets. They were needed in this dusty house. She went over and inspected them. All

Anthony Henry novels – the twins of those in her father's office. She took the teacup off the stack and lifted the top book up. It was one of the few that Kaela had read. She had been surprised by it. A British author had sided with South Africa in a war between the two countries. It was almost like the British author *preferred* the South African army.

She opened the book to the back cover and stared at the author's photo.

It was old man Henry.

Forty years younger.

Kaela quickly stood and stared up at the mantelpiece. Writing award after writing award lined the wooden shelf. There was even a famous movie award. Framed bestseller lists from the 1970s dotted the walls.

"You are Anthony Henry!" she screamed.

"Well spotted."

"You are one of the most famous authors in the world. There are actors who owe their entire careers to you. My father has every single one of your books. You saved him in England."

"My, how heroic of me."

He walked over and gave her the note, she took it as though it was made of stars.

"Make sure you give that to my neighbour. I'm tired of these unruly children and that ravenous donkey who never tires of destroying my plants."

"Why are you here?"

"I live here, why are you still here?"

"I mean, why are you in South Africa? Why aren't you living the high life in London?"

"Because nobody thinks to look for me here."

"Who looks for you?"

"Everybody. Now please go back to the stable, your incessant questions are doing more damage to my day than that donkey did to my begonias."

Kaela left before he pushed her out. She ran all the way back to the stables.

"He's Anthony Henry. He is Anthony Henry!"

No one knew what she was talking about.

"Old man Henry! He is one of the most successful authors in the world. My favourite actor has a career only because of his books."

"How much sugar have you had?" Jasmyn asked.

"None. He's Anthony Henry."

"What would a world-famous author be doing in Port St. Christopher?" Emily asked.

Kaela thought about his books, they were all about South African history.

"He loves South Africa. That's why he's hiding here."

"You mean to tell us that there's an award-winning author right next door, and he's been here for years?" Russell asked.

"Yes."

They all looked over at old man Henry's house.

It seemed to stare back and them and smile.

They all shivered.

Trixie misjudged the jump and went down too low. Siren's neck came up and whacked her face.

"Trixie, you are jumping a three-foot jump as though it was nine feet high," Bart said.

Trixie wanted to scream: What does it matter? Siren doesn't need to know how to jump.

"Bella, you're up."

"Come on, KaPoe, let's show Siren how it's done."

Trixie rolled her eyes, and then rolled them back again when Bella and KaPoe flew over the jump.

Every other intermediate rider had another turn. They all jumped without a problem. Even Kaela and Spirit.

"Trixie, wanna try again?" Bart asked.

Bella snorted, "*Try* being the operative word."

Trixie brought Siren around, nudged him into a canter, pointed him towards the jump and gave him rein. He changed direction and cantered around the jump.

Bella laughed.

"Trix, he has too much rein and your canter is too slow. He doesn't have enough power to lift," Bart said.

"He has a slow canter because I've taught him to canter slowly. I need it for dressage."

"Yes, but it doesn't serve you when you need to jump."

"I *don't* need to jump!" Trixie shrieked.

Bart recoiled at the bite in her voice.

"I think it is a case of her not knowing how to get Siren to jump," Bella said.

"Oh shut up, Bella!" Trixie screamed, "If you think you are so flaming brilliant, you come jump him."

"I'm not jumping your horse."

"Yes, because you are too scared. You are all talk and no action."

"Oh, I can jump that fleabag."

"Come on then, let's see it."

Bella shook her head.

"Jump him, Bella," Bart instructed, "If you are so sure you can, then do it."

Trixie dismounted. Bella slowly dismounted and handed KaPoe's reins to Bart. She walked over to Siren and mounted him.

Siren's ears automatically went back. He stomped his foot and tried to whip Bella with his tail.

"Well then, jump," Trixie said, "I'm waiting."

Bella scowled at her and nudged Siren, who backed up.

"Go forward," she cried.

"Are you going to jump him backwards?" Trixie asked.

"Everyone, get your cameras ready," Kaela said.

Finally, Bella got Siren in line with the jump but he refused to move, throwing his head every time she kicked.

"Any time this century, Bella," Trixie said.

But Siren wouldn't move, and eventually reared in an attempt to get Bella off.

Trixie raced over to Bart, mounted KaPoe, nudged him towards to the jump, and sat deeply in the saddle as he cantered over. She gave him rein and went down as he jumped. She landed easily on the other side. The intermediates clapped for her.

"So what?" Bella spat, "That means you can get KaPoe to jump. You still can't get Siren to jump properly."

"No," Trixie snapped, "That means that you have a push-button horse and can't ride properly when you are on any other horse."

The intermediates clapped again.

Bella dismounted and threw the reins at Bart, "Get off my horse," she screamed at Trixie.

Trixie dismounted and walked over to Bart and Siren. Kaela rode Spirit up to them, dismounted, handed the reins to Bart and mounted Siren. She gathered up the reins and nudged him into a canter; she rode him once around the ring, and then brought him into the jump. He cleared it perfectly.

Trixie swallowed her jealousy, and silently willed Kaela to get off her horse!

"Wow, women!" Bart said. "You lot are scarier than the Grim Reaper with a cold after his mother shrunk his cloak in the wash."

❧ Seven ❧

"So, first, her lead actress breaks her ankle. Then, her lead actor gets food poisoning. Then, her lead alien gets chickenpox. Then, the stage gets termites. Then, it rains on a few of the outfits and they get mouldy. Then, her brother – who is the director – inexplicably loses his voice."

Bart looked at Kaela with big eyes, "That play is cursed."

"It's because she wondered out loud what more could go wrong," Angela said from the saddle.

"She jinxed herself," Björn agreed. "Just make sure you don't wear green when talking to her."

"Three-and-a-half feet," Bart said, and gestured to the jump.

"Easy," Angela said.

Bart went to join Kaela and Björn, who were sitting on the wooden fence to watch Angela practise for the Superius test the next day.

"I *still* think that horse is too small," Bart said.

"Well there is no one else to ride who can handle the crowds at Equestrian International."

"Spirit is a descendant of a world-record-holding horse," Kaela said.

"Spirit is not Time Traveller," Angela said and cantered around the ring. She brought Dawn over the jump without a problem.

"That horse can fly," Bart said as he jumped down and walked over to the jump. He lifted the pole to the next catch, "Four feet."

"Easy."

Angela cleared that jump too. And four-and-a-quarter feet.

"Okay, second highest it can go. Four-and-a-half feet. But trust me, that is *far* from as high as it could go."

"I thought it was the first time Equestrian International had done this."

"It is," Bart said as he climbed the fence.

"So how do you know how high the jump gets?"

"I've seen it in the Empire Games."

"But those are professional riders, of course they are going to be able to jump eight-and-a-half feet," Kaela said.

Bart shrugged, "Don't assume the jump won't get that high. South African professional riders start *out* at Equestrian International. The jump is going to get *high*. All of the riding schools in Natal have been invited."

"All of them?" Angela asked.

Bart nodded.

"Even Sagittarius Stables?"

Bart nodded.

Angela went white, her hands began shaking on the reins. Dawn threw her head back.

"Are you going to jump?" Bart asked.

Angela nodded, nudged Dawn, cantered around the ring and brought her towards the jump. She did not give enough rein and went down at the wrong moment. There was too much weight on Dawn's neck and not enough room to stretch. She came down on the jump and it crashed down to the ground.

"Are you sure you don't want to ride Spirit?" Bart asked.

Angela shook her head, "That was my fault, not hers. She has jumped higher than this."

Angela dismounted and landed on shaky legs. Björn walked around Dawn's head.

"What is Sagittarius?"

"My old stable."

"I'm sure that Jemimah Duck woman won't be there."

"Her name was Gemma. And she might be."

Björn pulled his mobile from his back pocket, "I'll check out Equestrian International's website and see who is representing Sagittarius."

She nodded and walked Dawn to the stall. She untacked the horse with trembling hands. She could not face any

Sagittarius rider, let alone Gemma. She would just have to tell Wendy that Bart would have to do the Superius test. Or Kaela. Or any other jumper.

"Knock, knock," Kaela said as she came to the stall. "So what are plans for tomorrow? Are they interviewing you before you jump?"

Angela closed her eyes and put her face in her hands, "I completely forgot about that. I haven't even told my parents yet."

Kaela shrugged, "I'll tell your mom while they are interviewing you. She can hardly kill me can she?"

"No don't, I don't want to deal with it right now" said Angela into her hands. She looked up, "I don't want to do it."

"Do what?"

"Jump."

Kaela looked at her in surprise, "Because you knocked the jump over? That's the first time I've seen you do that. You'll be fine tomorrow."

"No, because Sagittarius Stables will be there."

Kaela frowned, rolled her eyes and waved her hand through the air, "Don't worry about them. They will probably send the catty brat they usually send. But she's easily beaten. Her ego is bigger than her talent."

"What catty brat?"

"Gemma Larkin."

"You *know* Gemma?"

90

Kaela shrugged, "About as well as anyone knows a hobgoblin."

"How do you know her?"

"She competes with Sagittarius. She will be at Pignut Spinney. When I kick her butt, it will be the tenth time in my life. And yet Sagittarius maintains that she's their best jumper. Except for this one other girl who won everything at Equestrian International but doesn't ride at Sagitt– oh my word, it's you!" Kaela put her hands over her mouth. "You know since you left, she's been going around saying she's the best rider."

"How do you know this?"

"I'm friends with her on LetsChat. How else can I show off every time I beat her? Keep your friends close but your enemies closer."

Björn walked up the stall, his face was pale.

"Uhm, I just looked at the list of riders," he said, "Gemma Larkin is listed under Sagittarius Stables."

Angela's heart stopped beating; she began shaking her head, "I can't jump tomorrow. I can't be interviewed. I can't. I can't. I can't."

"You will beat her *easily*," Kaela said.

"It's not that. I just can't be near her."

"But we'll be there with you tomorrow," Björn said, "I'll push her in the mud if she dares go near you."

"You want me to punch her? I will. My father teaches me to punch every Tuesday night. I could probably take her two front teeth out," Kaela said hopefully.

"No," Angela said in an odd voice, she was beginning to turn green, "I can't ride tomorrow."

She raced out of the stall and down into the practice ring where she collapsed into the dust.

Björn made a move to follow her. But Kaela stopped him.

"No one wants to see their boyfriend after they have just puked. Go find Bart and tell him he may be stepping in tomorrow."

"Come on, Siren. We aren't going to get blue next week if this is what we're presenting. Where is your former smugness? Where's mine?"

Trixie tried once more to do the dressage exercise she would need to do at Pignut Spinney, but, as before, she failed. She could almost see that blue ribbon wave goodbye and flap off towards the horizon.

She sighed, leaned down onto Siren's neck, and just breathed in.

"Could it be that you are trying too much and forgetting your love of the sport?"

"Hello Finley."

"Well hello there. Would you like to go for an outride?"

She sat up straight and looked over, "As long as I don't have to do dressage."

She never thought she would say those words. How far she had fallen!

Five minutes later both Finley and Jester led the way out of Apley Towers.

"Where are we going?"

Finley shrugged, "I don't know. Maybe we'll know when we get there."

"What a fabulous way to live. I couldn't live that way, But it's still fabulous."

"Why are you overworking Siren?"

"Because we need to win at Pignut Spinney. It's our first show, the first time I'm not competing in jumping, the first time I decide my own fate."

"So you need to show everyone that you are better for choosing your own path?"

"Something like that."

Finley lifted one eyebrow, "So what happens if you don't win?"

"I will," Trixie said, with more confidence than she felt.

"What do you care what other people think?"

"I don't."

Finley laughed, "Obviously you do."

"Well I want everyone to know that Siren was the right choice for me."

"What does it matter what anyone else knows? As long as you know it, who cares what everyone else thinks?"

Trixie sighed, "Also a very good way to live. Not for me.

But a very good way."

The two were quiet as they made their way down a footpath through the tall trees. Monkeys chattered to them loudly and bushbabies stared at them with eyes far too big for their heads.

"Where does this lead?" Trixie asked.

"I don't know," Finley said as though he did.

Siren climbed the dune, stopping to sniff at the green gunk on the sand.

"Is that seaweed?" Trixie asked.

"Yes, it's low tide. It got left behind."

"Apley Towers is *not* this close to the beach."

"Not by road, no. But if you know the secrets …"

They reached the top of the hill and stared out onto the ocean. The small waves glistened like sapphires under the dazzling sun. The white sand sparkled like glitter. The salty smell of the Indian Ocean danced around her head and through her hair.

"If you know the secrets, you can find the magic," Finley said, and he nudged Jester down the hill.

Trixie smiled and followed him. This was obviously Siren's first time on a beach. He stared in wonder at the ocean, and got a fright when his hooves sank into the sand.

Trixie encouraged him and soon he was walking across the beach like a pro.

"So, tell me all the secrets," she said as she came up beside Finley.

"Well, firstly, horse riding is for fun. If you're not having fun, then there is no point. If you have a horrible week with Siren, ruin your relationship, and put it in his head that shows are bad, is it really worth a blue ribbon?"

"No, not at all."

Finley nodded, "The secret is to be happy. Are you happy with the way things usually are?"

"Yes. We have fun together."

"Isn't that worth more than all the blue ribbons in the world?"

Trixie smiled as Siren jumped when the sea water touched him. He neighed loudly, stopped walking, and began using his front hooves to dig at the sand and slosh the water around.

"Yes," Trixie laughed, "his happiness is worth more than a billion blue ribbons."

"Worth more than the opinion of others too," Finley said and brought Jester around Siren and halted him next to Trixie.

The horses stood tail to nose while the humans stared at each other.

"Any other secrets?" Trixie asked.

"Yes," Finley said and gestured for Trixie to lean in close.

She leaned towards him, he put his hand under her chin and tilted her head up. He kissed her and then pulled away, "Isn't it better not knowing how the story ends?"

Trixie searched her brain for every cheeky or sarcastic answer she had, it was blank.

Instead she kissed him back.

"We're going to have to get off this beach before someone comes. Horses aren't allowed here," Finley said.

Trixie nodded and led Siren back up the hill. She turned to look at the ocean one last time before disappearing down the trail again.

They knew there was trouble as soon as they were through Apley's gates. Leo Willoughby's car was in front of Wendy's house and Björn sat on the front steps looking ashen-faced and jolted.

"What's happened?" Finley asked.

"Why is Mr Willoughby here? Is Kaela okay?" Trixie asked.

Björn nodded, "Kaela called him. Angela had a bit of a meltdown."

"What?"

"She's inside."

Trixie dismounted and handed Siren's reins to Finley, she raced past Björn and up the stairs. She pounded through the door, making everyone jump.

"What happened?" she asked as she raced to the couch.

Kaela and Angela were already seated. In the kitchen, Trixie could see Leo making some sort of drink. Trixie sat down on the other side of Angela. She was much paler than usual and trembling.

Kaela gave a look over Angela's head that said not to say anything.

Wendy came into the room and handed an envelope to Kaela, "Now that Trixie is here, you can give this to my neighbour."

"What is it?" Kaela asked as she reluctantly took it and stood up.

"It's a cheque for the window."

"He is a multi-millionaire, why can't he pay for the window himself? It's not like he has anything else to spend his money on. Except maybe a psychologist with a specialist degree in hoarding."

"It doesn't matter, it's the principle of the thing. Now please go before the sun sets and you have to be alone with him at night."

Wendy showed her teeth.

"So you think he is a vampire too?"

"The only vampire is Gemma Larkin," Angela said softly.

Trixie frowned at her.

As Kaela left the room her father entered it. He knelt in front of Angela and gave her the drink he had made.

"It's chamomile tea, it will do you good," he said.

She nodded and took it.

"Sip slowly, your puke would not go well with Wendy's décor."

Trixie laughed, Angela smiled, Leo tucked his long hair behind his ear.

"What's going on with you, Angela?" he asked softly.

Angela shrugged and took another sip, her colour had

come back and she was no longer trembling.

"A bully from my past just came back into my life."

"Gemma Larkin?" Trixie asked. "She's not a bully. She is a fluffed-up plastic doll who can't even ride properly. I had a broken arm once and still managed to beat her."

Leo held up his hand for silence. Trixie snapped her mouth shut.

"How is she back in your life?"

Tears sprang to Angela's eyes, "She's competing against me tomorrow."

"But that is only for one day, and you don't have to see her or talk to her. Both Kaela and Trixie will be there."

He looked over at Trixie who quickly nodded, "I'll beat her with my crop if you want."

"Let's not go that far," Leo said.

"We may have to stop Kaela. She usually wants to beat Gemma up anyway. She's just looking for an excuse to whack her."

Angela smiled and downed the last of her drink.

"Do you feel better about tomorrow?" Leo asked.

Angela looked at the ground and shook her head, "It doesn't matter if she doesn't get near me. What happens if I don't win? What is she going to think?"

"I don't understand," Leo said.

"She thinks she is a better rider than me, and she always tried to turn people against me. If I made the smallest mistake they all used to laugh at me and mock me. And it made me make more mistakes. So tomorrow, if I don't win, they will all think it is because I'm a bad rider and they will laugh at me."

"She sounds like a very sad and lonely person with nothing and no one. She feels so terrible about herself that she has to bring other people down. People like her should not be feared, they should be pitied."

"Yeah, I agree. She is like a worse version of Bella. You would think the two of them would be friends but they hate each other," Trixie said.

Leo put his hand up again. Trixie took the hint and stopped talking.

"It doesn't matter what she is," Angela said quietly, "it's what she thinks. I have to show her that I am a better rider than her, or she will think I am a total loser. Maybe I am."

Trixie breathed deeply, she had the same problem.

Leo looked from one girl to the other, "The wolf does not care what the sheep think."

Kaela stomped her way up the stairs and banged the knocker loudly. She had never been impressed by Anthony's books, but she was less than impressed by his surly demeanour. She heard him shuffling towards the door and wondered how old he really was.

"You're back?" he asked as he opened the door.

She handed him his cheque, "From Wendy," she said.

She turned to leave.

"You said you were a Willoughby?"

She turned back towards him, "Yes, I'm Kaela Willoughby."

He nodded slowly, "A Willoughby with such an intriguing grasp of language."

She sighed, "Yes, a Willoughby with such a grasp of language. But please, Mr Henry, tell me what exactly a name has to do with anything? A rose by any other name would still smell as sweet. I am also a Darling, a Fraser, a Pepler, a Thompson and a Crocker. What does being a Willoughby have anything to do with anything?"

Anthony's eyebrows rose and he smirked, "It's an interesting surname on a girl in Port St. Christopher who can quote Shakespeare off the top of her head."

"It is a series of coincidences. I inherited it from my father, who inherited it from his. Nothing out of the ordinary."

Anthony nodded, "Would that father be Vernon, Owen or Leo?"

Kaela's breath caught in her throat at the mention of her father and uncles, "Leo. But how do you know their names?"

Anthony smiled, revealing yellowing teeth with a gold bar in the bottom row, "Because she dedicated her books to each of her sons."

"Who?"

"Lavinia Willoughby."

Kaela frowned at him, "My middle name is Lavinia. I'm named after my grandmother."

Anthony nodded and gestured for her to come in. She followed him in shock. He grabbed a book from one of the many shelves and handed it to her. It was white with purple writing that said *The Wolf's Secrets* in a font that looked like lipstick. The name Lavinia Willoughby was written on the bottom in cursive.

She turned the book over and looked at the author's photo. She had seen it before. It was framed and sitting on the lid of the grand piano on the Willoughby farm. It was a picture of her grandmother taken in the 1960s, before she became a wife and mother. Kaela opened the book and read the dedication:

To my third baby, Leo.
You never slept and only ever wanted to be on my lap.
And so, you forced me to write this book.
May you always be as lovely as you are now.

Kaela looked up at Anthony with wide eyes, "She was an author?"

He nodded, "Quite a successful author. Look at the list of all her books."

Kaela turned the page over and stared in shock at the list. It covered two pages. She snapped the book shut.

"How did you know she was my grandmother?"

Anthony laughed, "She was always my favourite author. I lived for her work. She was born and grew up in the same English town I grew up in. And one day, without warning, she up and moved to South Africa. That was quite a shock for me. I was born in Port St. Christopher and the fact that she was down here intrigued me. It pushed me to write my first book about Bartholomew Diaz."

"But she didn't live here. They had a farm in the Midlands."

"She lived here first. Why do you think her sons built their businesses here? It is in their souls."

"But how did you know I was her granddaughter?"

"Your surname. The way you speak. You sound exactly like her. There were too many coincidences. Go on, read a line."

Kaela opened the book at random:

Elizabeth knew that a simple series of accidents had led her here. But that didn't mean she would not take advantage of all that she had found. After all, the wolf makes her own way and doesn't bother with the opinions of others.

She snapped the book shut again and put it on the table, "I have to go."

She raced out of the house, back through the garden and into Apley. She stormed up the stairs and through the door.

"Where's my father?" she screamed.

Trixie and Angela looked at her with big eyes.

"Somebody is in trouble," Bart teased.

"What is it?" Leo asked as he came out of the kitchen.

The smile fell from his lips under the glare of Kaela. He took a step back.

"She was an author?" Kaela screamed, "The whole time she was an author? For years you knew I wanted to be an author, and my own grandmother used to dominate the market. And you didn't say anything. The whole time. You just left me to bumble through trying to figure what to do, meanwhile you knew. You knew. And you lied!"

She turned and ran out of the house, her blood pumping loudly in her ears, red, hot rage across her face. She was more angry than she had ever been in her life. She didn't know where she was going but she walked quickly.

Hopefully if she walked quick enough she could walk off the edge of the planet, and spend the rest of her life floating in space.

⚚ Eight ⚚

Angela looked around Equestrian International and gulped. This place usually made her feel powerful: she was their three-time champion after all. But today it made her feel small and exposed. It didn't help that her Apley Towers tie was borrowed from Bart as she had not bought her own yet, and everyone had only remembered she needed the tie that morning. It would be the first time she had ever competed with a boy's tie. A judge had already mentioned that she would probably start a new fashion, but for Angela the tie meant just one more thing that could be mocked.

"Dawn, keep still," she said as she tried to do the girth. The mare kept skipping sideways and ripping the buckles out of Angela's hands. Eventually Angela put her head back and sighed, she would have to ask someone else to do it as her nerves were affecting her horse.

"Great, I can't even tack my own horse now."

"That doesn't surprise me," a voice said.

Angela turned to face the stall door, and her blood turned to ice. Gemma Larkin stood there and smiled.

"Hello Angela. Thankfully, it's been a while. I hope you've been better than you were. Since you left Sagittarius, we have all been super happy."

Angela's tongue turned into a sponge, she couldn't form a sentence. This made Gemma's smile wider.

"You are so brave to ride such a small horse in a height competition. I would never, but then it seems like I actually understand the principle of the test. Have Equestrian International indicated how disappointed they are with their champion's poor choices?" She smiled and pushed herself away from the door, "See you in the ring."

Angela watched her walk off over to her friends and start talking. The three of them turned to look at Angela, then they all looked at each other and laughed.

Hot tears stung Angela's eyes. She quickly wiped them away as she heard Trixie and Kaela walk up.

"So you just ignored your dad the whole night?" Trixie asked.

Kaela nodded, "I told my gran to keep him away from me. She thinks I'm being an overdramatic diva. She says I should have just researched Lavinia and found out on my own. But honestly, who in the world researches their ancestors?"

"I try not to," Angela said in a shaking voice.

Kaela turned to Trixie, "Have you ever researched your ancestors?"

Trixie shook her head.

"Could one of you please do the girth?" Angela asked, "I'm too nervous and I'm affecting her."

Trixie came around and grabbed the buckles. Dawn stood perfectly still and allowed Trixie to adjust the girth and push down on the stirrup to test it.

"Perfect," she said.

"Thank you," Angela said, and stroked Dawn's long sleek neck. The three girls had scrubbed the horse until she shone. They had also plaited Dawn's mane and tail. And despite it being unconventional, a small iron feather had been plaited into her tail at the request of Phoenix.

"We're all here for you now," Kaela said and she ran her fingertips over the feather.

Angela looked at the feather and nodded.

"Such a pity Phoenix's lead understudy fell into the tank at the aquarium," Angela said.

"Such a pity there wasn't water in it to break her fall," Trixie added.

It was official: Phoenix's play was cursed.

"Who is acting as her lead now?"

"Phoenix," Trixie and Kaela said together.

"Writer turned actress, isn't it usually the other way around?"

"Would the representative of Apley Towers sign in?" a voice on the intercom said.

Angela's stomach somersaulted, she couldn't face Gemma again.

"One of you has to come with me."

Trixie looked at Kaela, "You warm Dawn up. I'll deal with Gemma."

Kaela nodded.

"Don't overwork her," said Angela.

The two walked off in the direction of the judge's table.

"Is that Bella?" Trixie asked as she pointed to a girl hanging onto a professionally dressed rider. "Does she have a boyfriend?"

"Yes!" Angela cried, "She was talking on the phone about her new boyfriend a couple of weeks ago."

"There is a man who would love her for more than a day?"

Trixie and Angela stopped in shock as the rider turned to face them.

It was Jason.

Jason was a rider from Barren Hollow who had been the object of Bella's fascination for years.

"How did she wear him down?" Trixie asked.

"Proof that love is blind."

"And deaf, and dumb, and stupid."

Angela ignored Bella and went to sign her name on the list.

"Well hello again, Angela May."

Angela dropped the pen and began to tremble.

"Hi Gemma," she said quietly.

Trixie raced over and stood in front of Angela. Gemma

scowled and looked Trixie up and down.

"I see you're not representing Apley Towers this time, Beatrix."

"A stable only needs one representative and since Angela is the best there is, she is our representative," Trixie said coolly.

Gemma snorted.

"I see Sagittarius didn't read the memo that told them to send their best rider," Bella added.

Angela looked over, even more shocked that Bella was insulting Gemma than she had been about the fact that Bella had a boyfriend.

"I am the best at Sagittarius."

Bella snorted, "Oh you must be joking. The only reason you are here is because your mother owns the riding school."

Gemma paled.

"And it's such a pity she didn't pass any of her riding skills down," Bella said.

Gemma lifted one eyebrow, "Nice boyfriend, Sibella, shopping at second-hand stores is so last year." She looked over at Jason, "When you are bored of her you can always come back to me. Oh, and Angela, nice tie. I would never be brave enough to dress like a man."

With that she turned and sauntered off. The judge let her breath out in a loud whoosh, "Wow. That was more exciting than a soap opera."

Jason looked around then leant over to Angela and Trixie,

"Just be warned, she has a new horse. He is a retired show jumper. He won bronze in the Empire Games two years ago."

Angela closed her eyes and put her head against Trixie's back.

"Once again, mommy *buys* her way to the top," Bella said.

Angela glanced over at Bella, who looked from Jason to Angela and said, "Well one of you needs to beat her."

"Let's get back to Kaela before I start liking Bella," Trixie whispered.

"She was almost defending me against Gemma," Angela said as they walked off.

I thought she didn't like me.

"Don't look too much into it. Bella just doesn't like her Biggest Stable Bully reputation to be brought into question. She always ignores us and bullies Gemma when they are near each other. She'll be back to bullying you on Monday."

Angela sighed, "Oh great."

"They are just jealous of you," Kaela said when the girls had told her what happened, "you make them both insecure."

"They make *me* insecure," Angela whined.

"So ignore them and focus on the competition," Trixie said.

"Do I really look like a man?" she asked, and touched her tie.

Trixie stared at her with a frown, "You are a bit too pretty to be a man."

"I wouldn't go on a date with you, that's for sure," Kaela said, "I like my men sarcastic, rustic and wee bit on the difficult side."

"You just described your father," Trixie said.

Kaela scowled at her.

"I love the tie, Angela," said Cecilia, one of the owners of Equestrian International as she walked past, "are you trying to break the moulds of what women are expected to wear by throwing out the female tie and embracing a unisex uniform?"

"Yes, she is," Kaela quickly said, "We are hoping for a unisex tie by the end of the Season."

Cecilia nodded knowingly, "That's fabulous, I love it. You girls truly are the future of riding." She smiled and walked away.

"I wouldn't go on a date with her either," Trixie said, "she scares me."

"She looks way too deeply into things," Kaela said with wide eyes, "Like an English teacher … or Tessigan."

Ten minutes later Angela sat in the saddle and stared as they put the jump up. It was shaped and decorated like a brick wall, but made entirely of foam.

It was a giant sponge.

According to the announcer, the jump sometimes got so high that horses simply crashed into it. Anything but foam would do even the tallest horses damage.

The jump started at two feet and Angela, as champion, was invited to go first.

She cleared it to cheering crowds. The rest of the schools followed. No one was eliminated. The jump was then raised to two-and-a-quarter feet. Once again, all the riders jumped without a problem. Kaela and Trixie, assuming the title of bodyguards, kept close to Angela when she wasn't riding. Bella, assuming a title all of her own, never ventured far from Jason. The two-and-a-half feet and two-and-three-quarter feet jumps proved a bit more challenging for the less experienced riders, but everyone made it over the jumps without knocking the bricks.

By the time the jump got to three feet, the crowds had begun to calm down. The jump was starting to get quite high. The first rider to be eliminated was from a school the girls had never heard of. The rider jumped too low, knocking the top layer of bricks down. He exited the ring to applause.

"Once he gets around the corner he is going to burst into tears," Kaela said.

At three-and-a-quarter feet, three more riders were eliminated, including the rider from Pignut Spinney.

Angela watched Gemma and her horse, Empire Gold, enter the ring.

"Fall, fall, fall," Kaela whispered.

But Gemma didn't. If anything, she barely looked like she had been working.

"Oh the benefits of a push-button horse," Trixie sneered.

The jump was then raised to three-and-a-half feet, and eliminated six more riders. Angela, a veteran of show jumping, understood that it was essentially the horse who was eliminating these riders. They were not jumping as they should have been taught, they were misjudging the height or not stretching their necks far enough.

Angela instinctively understood that a Superius test had to have a specific horse to conquer it. Although Dawn very rarely lost jumping competitions, Angela had to wonder if she was the right type of horse for this specific competition.

At the Empire Games there always seemed to be a fire burning in the horses who won this competition … They seemed, in spirit, to be bigger than the task they were being asked to perform.

Dawn was not like that.

Angela smiled and patted her horse, she wouldn't have her any other way though.

At three-and-three-quarter feet there were only Angela, Jason, Gemma, and the rider from Equestrian International left.

"And then only the best were left," Trixie said.

Because the riders and their horses kept disappearing, the crowd and protection around Angela disappeared too. Before the kodas had realised it, Gemma was next to them. Her horse towered over Dawn.

"You are so brave, Angela. I don't know how you are going to get that tiny horse over those bricks. You are much braver than anyone who brought tall horses" she said. "Or maybe you are not so much brave as foolish."

Kaela looked at Gemma, "Don't you have other people to bug?"

Gemma looked directly at Angela who tried her hardest to ignore the stare, "Are they going to talk for you all day? I wish I was rich enough to hire people to think for me. If only we were all so lucky."

Bella laughed, "You definitely need someone to think for you."

"Don't you have better places to be, Gemma?" Jason asked. "You are clearly not wanted here."

Gemma shut her mouth and went red in the face.

Angela looked at him and smiled. He rolled his eyes and shook his head. Angela thought he had very odd taste when it came to women.

Three-and-three-quarter feet knocked Jason out.

"And then there were three," said Kaela.

Angela, Gemma and the rider from Equestrian International stared into the ring as they put the jump up to four feet.

The bricks were a deep red colour as opposed to the brown of the ones beneath it. Almost as though it was warning.

Angela had to jump first. She could do it. She knew she could. She had done it as recently as the day before.

"Good luck Angela," Gemma said, "I hope you can get that midget over the jump."

"Come on Angela," Kaela cried, "Show the world what that midget horse can do."

"Yeah Angela," Trixie said. "Show us why that midget horse is a *champion*."

As Angela rode into the ring she couldn't help but smile at that remark. Dawn was a champion. The crowd were cheering her because she was the favourite.

She gave her a pat on the neck, "Let's show these people how you fly."

The bell went and Angela nudged Dawn into a canter, they went once around the ring, took the first, smaller, practice jump and came around for the big one.

One, two, three strides: Angela leaned forward, put her hand flat against Dawn's neck and looked ahead. Dawn left the ground, tucked her front legs under her and sailed over the jump.

The crowd cheered loudly. Angela trotted Dawn back to Kaela and Trixie.

Kaela reached up and patted Dawn's neck, "All you need is fairy dust and good thoughts, and Dawn can fly!"

Gemma rolled her eyes.

Both Gemma and the other woman cleared the jump. And the four-and-a-quarter feet jump. The crowd were dead quiet now. It was as though the crowd thought, as one, that any noise may jinx the horses. No one wanted to be blamed for an elimination.

The jump was then put up to four-and-a-half feet.

Butterflies erupted across Angela's stomach. This was the height she had knocked down the day before.

"Remember Angela, the wolf does not care about the opinion of the sheep."

Angela nodded and nudged Dawn.

She waited for the bell.

"I am the wolf. I am the wolf," she chanted.

The bell went, and Angela kicked Dawn. The horse sprang into a canter. She was going faster than Angela usually allowed, but she needed the power to lift. They took the practice jump and rounded for the brick wall.

Dawn bolted, lifted and cleared it.

Trixie and Kaela cheered loudly. Angela sighed with relief. She wished Bart had been there to see it.

Next it was the turn of Equestrian International's rider. She let her horse go too fast, they knocked the practice jump and crashed through the foam wall. Her horse, terrified of the falling bricks bolted and almost galloped into the crowd. She got her horse under control a split second before his hooves left the ground to jump into the stand. The screaming crowds did not help the frightened horse.

"He doesn't understand that the wall isn't real," Trixie said, "he probably thought the bricks were going to crush him."

"Amateur," Gemma sneered.

The crowd cheered loudly for the horse and rider as they exited.

"And then there were two," Kaela said.

They rebuilt the jump and added another row.

Four-and-three-quarter feet.

The jump looked impossibly high. Angela nervously nudged Dawn into the ring. Angela knew her horse could fly, but she also knew those invisible wings had limitations. Without Angela on her back, Dawn would probably be able to get over this jump without a problem. But Angela added extra weight to be lifted. She wished she could get off and let Dawn jump alone. Well, honestly, if she was wishing for things, she wished she had taken Bart's advice and used another horse. A taller horse.

Dawn nickered and Angela smiled down at her, "I would rather be here with you than the tallest horse in the world," she said honestly.

She patted Dawn's neck and kicked her into action at the sound of the bell. Dawn raced around the ring, took the practice jump, rounded on the brick wall and soared over. The crowd gasped, went silent, and then cheered. Angela turned in the saddle to look at the jump. Two of the bricks were askew. She turned to the scoreboard to watch the replay of her jump. Dawn's front legs went over smoothly, but both back hooves knocked the bricks. They moved, wobbled but held. She wasn't eliminated, but she had hung on with the skin of her teeth.

Gemma and the very tall Empire Gold cleared the jump without trouble. He even seemed bored.

The jump was raised yet again. Five feet. Angela, on

horseback, would not have to lean down to touch it. Bile began to climb her throat, her head began to heat up under her hard hat. Her hands trembled on the reins. The security wall that went around her father's farm was shorter than this jump. It didn't have Gemma on the other side of it either.

Kaela grabbed Angela's ankle, she looked down, "The wolf does not care about the opinion of the sheep."

"You keep saying that as though it means something," Gemma said, "You should hire better people to think for you, Angela."

Trixie grabbed Angela's other ankle, "Do you want to know one of the secrets of life?"

Angela nodded.

"If it's not fun, it's not worth it."

Gemma snorted.

Angela nudged Dawn and they entered the ring to applause. Five feet was the highest she had ever attempted, and she had knocked the pole down. As they waited for the bell, Angela thought of the horse who had crashed through and panicked. Had he really thought it was a real wall? Had the act of falling into it traumatised him to such a point that he was no longer capable of discerning that human beings should not be jumped on? Was that horse now traumatised for life?

Beneath her, Dawn seemed to be made of electricity, and not the good kind. There was the kind of electricity that cooked a man's dinner and there was the other kind that cooked the man. Dawn seemed to be made of the latter.

Behind her, Gemma sat on an international champion. No matter how high Angela jumped Dawn, Gemma would jump Empire Gold higher.

The bell went and Angela nudged her horse. The electricity sprang forward. They cantered around the ring and took the practice jump. They rounded for the wall; Angela put up her hand and used the other one to jerk on the left rein. Dawn cantered around the wall. Angela's right hand was in the air, signalling that she resigned.

The crowd was quiet.

She slowed Dawn to a walk and made her way to her smiling friends.

Gemma pulled her horse in front of Dawn, "I told you I was the better rider."

Angela lifted one eyebrow the way her mother did when she had made a decision that was forbidden from being questioned, then she turned Dawn away and rode towards her friends.

The smirk dropped from Gemma's face, and she entered the ring to accept her award.

Angela dismounted and hugged Dawn.

"You did the right thing," Kaela said, "she would have crashed right through that jump."

"No award is worth that," Trixie added.

From deep within Dawn's neck, Angela said, "This wolf *does* care about the opinion of the horse."

᧒ Nine ᧖

The lights of the funfair greeted the group before they had even gotten inside. The cashier wrapped the yellow bracelets around each of their wrists and opened the gates for them.

"Where are we going first?" Björn asked.

"Nothing taller than five feet," Angela answered.

Trixie laughed a bit too loudly.

Tonight would be the first time she would see Finley since they had kissed. With all the stress of the competition out of the way, now she could actually think about it.

And when she did think about it, she couldn't stop smiling. She felt like she had a clothes hanger in her mouth.

"I want food first," Kaela said.

"You can't eat before you go on rides," said Björn.

"I can. Trixie can't."

Angela looked at Trixie.

"I like the rough rides," she said with a shrug.

The group made their way over to the food trucks.

"Yay! Veggie burgers!" Kaela cried.

Russell and Elizabeth were already there, sharing a plate of chips.

"You're eating?" Trixie asked him.

"Wow … How did you figure that out?" he answered.

"I mean *why* are you eating?"

Russell shrugged, "We were hungry."

"But what about the rides?"

Russell shrugged again. Trixie rolled her eyes. Once again, Russell was stepping out of the limelight in order to accommodate the not-so-bright sparkle of his girlfriend.

"You suck, Russell," Kaela said with a mouthful of veggie burger.

"Yeah, you two are the terror twins," Björn said, "You can't leave Trixie to go on the rough rides alone."

"She has Finley, she won't be alone."

"Finley might not like them," Trixie said irritably.

"What don't I like?" he asked as he walked up to them.

"Do you like the rough rides?" Trixie asked.

Her heart had suddenly started beating faster.

"I'll go on any ride but that one."

He turned and pointed to the biggest, brightest, loudest ride at the fair.

The ride Trixie couldn't wait to get on.

"I don't blame you, mate," Björn said, "that thing looks about as safe as sweating dynamite."

Kaela threw her rubbish away and turned to the group, "First, you *all* promised me I could take photos of you on the carousel."

The group groaned.

"Oi, you promised."

With much grumbling, they all made their way to the colourful ride. With the exception of Russell, who stayed behind with Elizabeth. Trixie mounted the purple horse and picked up the reins.

"I've always wanted to ride a purple."

"Purples are the best," Finley said as he got up onto the green horse next to her, "Mine is motion sick, I think."

Kaela stood in front of them with her camera, "Smile, or I will *make* you smile."

They both smiled and were then blinded by the flash.

"And it's a good thing I'm not directing this horse," Finley said as he rubbed his eyes.

"Would you crash?"

"We'd land up in the Pacific Ocean."

Trixie frowned, "The Pacific Ocean isn't anywhere near us."

"Exactly."

Trixie laughed as the ride started, knocking Kaela sideways into some unknown teenage boy who smiled and introduced himself and was quickly shoved sideways by his girlfriend.

Trixie would never admit it, but she actually enjoyed the slow, sweet pace of the carousel. The up-and-down rotating motion made her feel relaxed after the long day.

It also helped that Finley was next to her.

Once Kaela's desire for photos had been satisfied, Finley and Trixie escaped to experience the more daring rides. By the time they had gone through all of them twice and had found the group again, over an hour had passed.

"Have you had enough of an adrenaline fix yet?" Bart asked.

"For now," Trixie answered, "When did you get here?"

"Just after the carousel photo shoot," Bart said with a cheeky smile.

Trixie chuckled: poor Kaela, no one was particularly interested in her photo shoot.

Russell and Elizabeth had joined the group by this point as well.

"Have you gone on the big one yet?" Russell asked.

Trixie smiled at Finley, "No, my adrenalin junkie is being a wimp!"

Finley shrugged but gave her a smile.

Russell stared at the ride as the people on it screamed in terror.

"Wanna go on it with me, Russell?" Trixie asked.

He stared at the ride with longing.

The screaming stopped as the ride came to an end, letting off weary people who wobbled as they walked.

"Do it now, or forever wish you had," Kaela said.

"Okay," Russell said, "but we had better hurry up."

"Russell …" Elizabeth said with a frown.

"I'll be right back," he said, and began walking to the ride.

Trixie gave a quick wave to Finley and followed Russell.

"Come on!" she cried and pulled his arm.

They ran together, getting to the ride as it was closing. They sat down and buckled up.

"Don't puke," she said to him.

"I'll try not to."

The ride started by swinging them in an arc, then swinging them back. Holding them upside down and lifting them, only to drop them the next second. By the end they were swinging upside down.

It was only when they were safely back on the ground that Trixie realised she had been holding Russell's hand the entire time.

She looked at his face, illuminated in the bright green and blue lights.

And suddenly she realised why she was riding so badly in her pursuit for praise.

It turned out that there was one opinion that did matter to this wolf.

Russell's opinion.

The Ferris wheel lifted the carriage up, swinging it into the night. Kaela kept a death grip on the safety bar.

"You aren't going to fall," Bart said.

"And if I do?"

"I'm sure you'll fly."

Kaela kept her death grip.

When the carriage got to the very top, it stopped and rocked.

"Wow, you can see the whole of Port St. Christopher."

Kaela opened her eyes and looked around. On her left there was the darkness of the ocean, and on her right, the lights of the suburbs dotted through the trees.

"It looks so small," she said.

"And yet it is our entire world."

Kaela looked in the general direction of Apley. The darkness of the land showed where the horses roamed.

"Can I tell you a secret?" she whispered.

"Do I have to tell you one?"

"No, you can just owe me."

"Then yes, tell away."

"I've been thinking about the jump today. It got to five feet. Angela didn't jump it, but neither did Gemma."

"Gemma didn't need to. Angela resigned. Gemma won by default."

"That's not winning."

Bart shrugged, "That's the game, unfortunately."

Kaela nodded, "Do you think Spirit could jump that?"

Bart nodded, "Definitely. But Angela didn't want to jump him."

Kaela bit her bottom lip. The carriage began moving again and she instinctively grabbed Bart's arm.

"I don't mean Angela should have jumped Spirit. I mean, do you think I could jump that height?"

Bart looked at her, his eyes darting from one of her eyes to the other.

He slowly smiled, "I think you've jumped it before."

"When?"

"A few weeks ago. You jumped the fallen tree in the paddock."

"You saw that?"

Bart nodded, "I was watching you ride like you were racing Pegasus. I think you've already jumped that height – I'll measure that fallen tree to see how high it is. What are you planning?"

Kaela smiled, "What makes you think I'm planning anything?"

Bart smiled, "Because I know you."

Kaela laughed and leaned back.

"Nothing you do will change it," Bart said as he looked at her from the corner of the carriage, "Gemma will always be the winner."

"In the opinion of others."

"Yes, in the opinion of the ones who matter."

"Only Apley Towers matters," Kaela said as she stared at the moon, "and the people who are in it."

"All of them?"

"All of them," she tipped her head and looked at him, "we are a unit, even when we fight with each other. We are all one."

Bart smiled, "And when someone threatens those in our kingdom, do we act as a wolf pack and attack? Or are we werewolves, since you are so fond of the full moon and, of course, you're armed with bottled moonlight?"

Kaela laughed, "When did you invite yourself into my imaginary worlds?"

Bart dropped his eyes and smiled shyly, "I enjoy being there."

She looked up at the stars, "You have been in my kingdoms and the castles and the forests for so long, I don't even remember what they were like before you were there."

Bart shrugged and leaned his head against hers.

"I think I invited myself in on the very first day I ever saw you at the stable. You looked around and said 'This is Neverland', and I knew that for the rest of my life I would have one foot in another dimension. With you."

⤜ Ten ⤛

A very tired Phoenix stared out of the laptop screen.

"So how did the interview go? Were they disappointed that you resigned?"

"No, actually, not at all," Angela said, "the woman from Horse Masters said that it was the first time she had seen such a young rider make such a grown-up decision."

"So what was the interview about then?"

Angela shrugged, "The same old stuff to begin with: she just asked me questions about my riding history and my horses. But then she wanted to talk about why I decided to resign. And if I was happy with my decision. Oh, and about my tie – she wanted to know about my campaign for a unisex uniform."

"Thank you, Kaela." Phoenix laughed, "She's such an activist."

"Yeah, but now I am apparently at the forefront of the movement to abandon the girls' tie."

"They don't wear ties in England, you're just bringing South Africa in line with them."

"Oh, because that's less pressure than the other campaign," said Angela, rolling her eyes.

Phoenix laughed, "So, was resigning worth it?"

Angela nodded sadly, "It was *horrible* to lose to her. It felt like every bad thing she always said about me was right. But Dawn is more important. Dawn comes first." She shrugged, "I had to put myself aside for her."

Phoenix nodded knowingly, "When is the interview on TV?"

"Next week. The same day the other TV show is interviewing me at Apley."

"Wow, you're starting to get rather famous."

"Hopefully I can tell my parents what I did before it goes on TV."

Phoenix laughed.

"How's the play going?"

Phoenix sighed deeply, "I am honestly starting to believe it is cursed."

"Has something new happened?"

Phoenix sighed again, "One of my aliens fell into a patch of poison ivy, so now there is no original actor in any speaking role. *I'm* doing the lead, the understudies are doing the lead male and alien. There is no one left to do the last alien. Arion knows the lines so he could have done it, but he has no voice."

"How is he directing with no voice?"

"He carries a chalkboard around his neck. And now suddenly Satyr and Chiron can't read. Whenever he writes something for them, they pretend they can't read and accuse Arion of being insensitive to their disability."

Angela laughed, "Hopefully he has neat handwriting."

"It's Arion, of course he does – he makes a computer look sloppy."

"But wait a minute, isn't the other speaking alien the spaceship driver?"

Phoenix nodded.

"But Stella flirts with him, doesn't she?"

"Yes, she does. Which means I would have ended up flirting with my brother. So actually, I'm glad he has no voice."

"So go out there and pick a new actor who you will enjoy flirting with."

"There is no one I want to flirt with," Phoenix frowned and her eyes darted to the left.

"Really? Not even a man named Rowan Running Wolf?"

Phoenix's lips betrayed her. She couldn't hide her smile.

"Rowan is playing the alien?"

Phoenix nodded.

Trixie lifted her eyebrows, "Rowan Running Wolf, who

you are crushing on, is playing the alien that Stella spends the entire play flirting with?"

"Yes."

Trixie nodded in amusement, "Good move. Sounds like something I would do."

"You have a lot of explaining to do, what's with all these photos from the fair?"

"What about them?"

"Uhm, let's see. You and Finley on the carousel? Are we *still* maintaining we are just friends?"

"We are, yes."

Phoenix raised her eyebrows, "Yeah, right. Okay, but then tell me why there is then a photo of you and Russell *holding hands?*"

Trixie shrugged, "Kaela surprised us. She took a photo as the door opened."

"That doesn't explain *why* you were holding hands."

"It was a scary ride," said Trixie defensively.

"Sometimes I want to cut your head open and see your secrets."

Trixie didn't quite know whether or not Phoenix was joking.

"I don't like to talk about things because I don't like to jinx them."

"Sound advice," Phoenix said with a sigh, "Okay, what about this photo of Angela and Björn? It looks like it belongs in a magazine advert or something."

Trixie, who had been looking at that exact photo when

133

Phoenix phoned, smiled and said, "It was candid too. Björn had just got on the carousel horse behind Angela, and she turned to look at him. Kaela caught it."

"Speaking of Kaela, what's with her photo? Was there a romantic tryst at the top of the Ferris wheel?"

Trixie clicked onto the next photo: a selfie that Kaela and Bart had taken in the Ferris wheel carriage. They looked cosy and warm and happy.

"She said nothing happened and they were just chatting."

Phoenix nodded, "Will one of those two ever just tell the other how they feel?"

Trixie's jaw dropped, "Why do you believe Kaela when she says nothing happens, but not me?"

"Because Kaela can't keep secrets, and you are the queen of secrets."

Trixie sighed, she couldn't dispute that.

Kaela cycled into the garden just as the sun was rising. She had spent the night at Trixie's house, but it was time to face the music now. She couldn't avoid her father forever. She took her bike into the garage and went into the house. She wasn't surprised to see her father at the kitchen counter. Something had told her he would be there.

The two large piles of books on either side of him were a surprise though.

"Are you ready to talk?" he asked without looking up.

She knew he wanted her to apologise for screaming at him, but she couldn't do it. How could she apologise for the emotions he had set the stage for?

She put down her backpack, kicked off her shoes and went to the kitchen counter. She sat opposite him and took a sip of his hazelnut milk.

Leo gestured to the books, "These are all mum's books."

Kaela's eyes snapped from the piles to Leo. He had said the word 'mum'. Leo spoke so little of his own parents that she had never noticed him call his mother 'Mum', unlike other South Africans, who referred to their mothers as 'Mom'. Kaela's insides melted whenever Bart called his mother 'Mum'; was she noticing it simply because her father had put the harmony of the word in her head to begin with?

"I never told you she was an author because I didn't want you to feel as though you were hanging onto her coat-tails or had to follow in her footsteps at all. Most importantly, I didn't want you to think you had to battle her shadow."

"What do you mean, battle her shadow?"

Leo sighed, "I see it every day. When you come home covered in the stable and smelling like a horse, there is a moment when you walk through the door and I can literally see the words across your forehead, *Am I like her?*"

"Who?"

"Felicity."

Kaela's breath caught in her throat.

135

"I know, I can see it. You are battling your mother's shadow," Leo said. "You want to be known as the daughter of the great horse rider, but at the same time you want to make your own way in life."

She couldn't breathe.

He pointed to the ground, she turned to look at her shadow, "One of the things I can't help noticing these days is how much your shadow looks like Felicity. I drove past Apley last week, I saw you on this new horse. I was looking at you and him in the ring, and Felicity and Black Satin on the ground. That night you came home and I could see the question across your face."

Kaela swallowed her tears.

"You fight Felicity's shadow every day of your life. And some days you win, and some days you don't. That day I saw you at Apley, you weren't winning. I didn't want you to know about Mum's books because I didn't want you fighting a second shadow."

Kaela looked back down at her shadow and wondered if it was truly hers.

"I wanted there to be something in your life that was just yours. I wanted there to be something in your life where you walk your own path, not where you follow in our footsteps."

She slowly nodded, not trusting herself to speak.

"You used to know Mum was a writer. When she was still alive, she encouraged all your little stories. And then after she was gone, you seemed to forget. So I left you to forget.

I wanted you to be free. I wanted you to learn an important lesson without Mum's shadow hanging over you."

"What lesson?"

Leo leaned forward, "If you are not enough *without* the big publishing deals and the awards and the bestseller list, you will never be enough *with* it. You will *never* learn that lesson when it comes to your horse riding. No matter what you do, you are comparing yourself to Felicity. I wanted to spare you that with your writing."

Kaela nodded, "I'm sorry I yelled at you."

Leo took a sip of his hazelnut milk and shrugged, "It happens. I once yelled at my father about the herbal medicine he gave his cattle. One glance at my textbooks proved that he was right and I was wrong."

Kaela laughed, "That must have been embarrassing."

Leo smiled, "He didn't mention it. Just told me about the time he yelled at his father about the onions they were growing, then he dug them up and realised they weren't ready, just as his father had said."

Kaela laughed again.

Leo looked at his own shadow, "It's an interesting moment, I guess. When you realise your parents or your children are not an extension of yourself, and will do things differently."

"Would you give the cattle different medicine?"

"Yes, I would. But that doesn't mean my father was wrong. Would you have told your daughter about Lavinia?"

"Yes, I would have. But that doesn't mean my father was wrong."

"Well now that you know, don't let who she was control who you will be. Find your own path."

"Did she write fantasy?"

Leo shook his head.

"Well then, I'm already on my own path."

Leo smiled, "And as for giving you tips on how a writer's world works, I can't. I don't know. Mum never told me, and I didn't think to ask. Go ask Anthony Henry, he seems to enjoy telling you secrets."

"You knew he was living here?"

Leo nodded.

"So why aren't you more excited? He is your favourite author."

Leo shrugged, "He doesn't see me as Leo Willoughby. He sees me as Lavinia's youngest son, the son she dedicated her books to. I can't deal with that. He is doing to me exactly what everyone did to him enough times to drive him away from England."

Kaela reached over and picked one of the books up. It had a horse on the cover and a jumping circuit in the background.

"Kaela: *The Wise One*."

Leo nodded, "Kaela means 'the wise one' in Gaelic."

"I'm named after a horse?"

Leo shook his head, "You are named after a character in my favourite of Mum's books."

Kaela opened the book to the dedication page.

To Leo,
I promised you a story about an amazing
woman.
I hope Kaela is good enough.

"What's it about?"

"A very difficult competition on a mysterious horse," Leo said. "Read it."

She shut the book, "I would rather not know how it ends. It's more exciting that way."

Leo nodded.

Kaela put the book back and ran her hands over the rest of them, "She managed to write all of these with three sons and a farm to run?"

"Most of them. Some were written before she was married or even in South Africa."

Kaela smiled, "That gives me a lot of hope."

"About what?"

"About managing to write books while having a family and running my own stable. You worried me the other night when you said I needed to get everything done *before* I have a family. I thought I might have to choose one or the other."

Leo looked at the books, "Obviously not. I'm glad Mum carried on writing after we were born. It gave me a good work ethic. I learnt very early on that nothing comes for free. You have to work hard for the good things."

Kaela found the book Anthony Henry had shown her, opened it to the dedication page, and showed it to Leo.

"And even if your baby doesn't sleep, good things still happen," she said.

"I agree. Thanks to my banana peel smoothie I've discovered a way to whiten teeth without poisonous chemicals."

"There's always a silver lining. You just have to look for it."

After Kaela showered, she went into her father's office, found what she was looking for, photocopied it, and left the house. She walked the path that led to Apley keeping an eye on her shadow, which danced in front of her.

She stopped and stared at it.

"Who are you?"

The shadow stared back.

Kaela sighed and carried on walking. She walked past Apley to Anthony Henry's house. She knocked on the door and waited for him to shuffle through the house.

"Is this the time to be showing up here?" he asked.

"I have something for you," she said calmly.

She would not let him bully her. She understood something about him now: Anthony Henry had not been enough before the adulations of writing, and now he was not enough with them. This made him angry with himself, not the world.

He held the door open for her and she went inside.

She looked at the bookshelves and wished she could run her hands over all of them. She wished she could soak in whatever it was that made them so magic.

"Sit down," he barked.

She went to the seat nearest the window so that she could see Apley. She smiled as she saw the rose bushes at the back of the garden, remembering how Angela had jumped the wall to steal one.

"What have you got?"

She handed him the sheet of paper and watched his face as he looked at it. It went from irritation to confusion.

"My grandfather took that photo of my grandmother and it has been in our house for years. I've never really paid attention to it. But now that I know she was an author, it makes a lot of sense."

The photo, which hung against the wall of Leo's study, was a black and white picture of Lavinia at the garden table. She was staring out into the horizon as though it held the secrets she searched for. In her hand was a pen and on her lap was a large notebook, written to nearly the back cover. On the back of the original, Kaela had been shocked to find that her grandfather had written, 'Lavinia Thompson writes her first bestseller as Lavinia Willoughby'.

That sentence had resonated deep within Kaela. How simple it was to be two people. She knew in her heart that she was both the granddaughter of an author, and that she had her own growing to do.

"I am going to be a writer," she said unapologetically, "And if I am not as successful as you or Lavinia, that is perfectly okay. Because I am also a rider, and if I am not as successful as Felicity Willoughby that is okay too. As long as I am good enough for me, that is all that matters."

Anthony Henry nodded, "Hold onto that thought in the dark days."

"I will, thank you."

She smiled; that was the first bit of writing advice she had been given.

And she hadn't even asked for it.

On the way home she watched her shadow. If she squinted her eyes and stood in a certain way, the shadow could be mistaken for her mother. She put her hand up and pretended to write. If she squinted really hard, the shadow could now be mistaken for her grandmother.

She un-squinted her eyes and sighed, then laughed.

The shadow on the ground was unmistakably Kaela.

❧ Eleven ❧

"How long does it have to cook for?" Angela asked.

"Until it smells and tastes right."

Björn came over, dipped a spoon in the sauce, blew on it and tasted it.

He shook his head, "Not quite."

"I can't believe you know how to cook," Angela said in shock.

"Why not?"

"Because you are a boy!"

"That's so sexist."

Angela shrugged helplessly, he had a good point.

"Okay, let's try a different angle, *why* do you know how to cook?"

"Because my mother abandoned us and my father couldn't cope. There was no one to look after me so I went with him to cooking classes. I'm probably the youngest person ever to make aubergine lasagne."

"Wow, impressive."

The two finished making dinner, set up the table, and generally tidied the house up. When Angela could see her father's car in the distance, Björn got his biking gear on and mounted his bike.

"Wish you could stay for dinner," Angela said.

"Only so that they don't kill you."

"No, because you cooked the dinner. You should stay to see their faces."

"You can tell me about it tomorrow."

Angela hugged him and rested her head against his shoulder. She breathed him in.

He kissed her on the temple, "Got to go, your dad is almost here."

She let go and handed his helmet over to him. He squeezed it on, waved goodbye, and drove off.

Within a minute her father pulled into the drive.

"Was that Björn I saw?" he asked as he climbed out of the car.

"Yes, he spent the afternoon here. Go wash up, dinner is ready. We're starting with roasted red pepper soup – made from scratch, and crusty bread – freshly baked."

George May's eyes went wide, "Dare I ask what the main course is?"

"French chicken in a white wine sauce on a bed of quinoa, mushrooms, green beans and grilled aubergine. Crème brulée for dessert."

"You cooked all that?"

"Nope, Björn did."

George whistled, "You found yourself a keeper."

They walked into the house. George stopped, stared, grabbed his mobile, and dialled his wife's number.

"Get here now. She cleaned and bribed her boyfriend to cook. There is obviously something wrong here. I am the father, I am not equipped to deal with this. Okay … okay," he disconnected the call, "She's on her way."

"I knew mom would be late, so I made you a few nibbles."

She went into the kitchen, picked up the cheese, apple, and grape platter and took it to her father.

"Is my kitchen in one piece?"

"Of course it is. You behave as though I destroy the kitchen every time I step into it. I'll admit, there was a slight mishap the last time I was in there. But now that the walls have been repainted and the ceiling light has been fixed, I think the kitchen and I have come to an understanding."

"And what understanding is that?"

"I understand that the kitchen is dangerous. And the kitchen understands why I invite Björn to cook."

Just as George finished the cheese platter, Gwendolyn pulled up. She had the same reaction to the house and dinner that George had had.

"Okay, what's happened? What have you broken?"

"You assume that I've broken something just because I've cleaned?"

Her parents stared at her warily as she dished the starters

up. They each took a tentative bite. The look of ecstasy on their faces was something Angela wished Björn had seen. They devoured starters, and waited not-so-patiently for the main course. Angela dished it up and watched in awe as her parents seemed to lose the ability to speak. All they could do was shovel the food into their mouths as quickly as possible.

Angela waited for them to finish the main course before talking to them.

"As you both know, my articles are gaining some ground on the horse circuits, and I have been invited to appear on two TV shows. I know you both believe that I shouldn't go on TV, and I respect that. But I believe that in order to have a career as a professional horse rider I need to make myself known."

"So you want our permission to do this?" George asked.

Angela breathed deeply, "Not quite."

Gwendolyn frowned.

"I've already had one interview. It will be on TV this weekend, and the other TV show will be interviewing me on Saturday."

"But your competition is on Saturday," Gwendolyn said.

"They are interviewing me before and after the competition, they're hoping to film me winning."

Angela looked from one parent to the other. She had expected a big reaction, but they both just stared sadly at her.

"Well, say something!" Angela said. "Yell at me, punish

me. Do something!"

"Yell at you for what?" Gwendolyn asked. "Making a career choice?"

"But you told me not to."

"No we didn't. We told you that we were worried about the TV coverage. We didn't say you couldn't do it."

"So why are you both looking at me like that? Like your hearts are breaking?"

"They are," George said. "Where's my little girl? Who is this career woman?"

"You're all grown up now," Gwendolyn said, "soon you'll fly the coop."

Angela laughed, "No I won't. Watching Björn cook taught me only one thing ... I'll never survive on my own. I'm living here until I'm old and grey."

George hiccupped and put his face in his hands.

"That is even worse news: I wanted to turn your room into a gym."

"Kaela, can I talk to you?"

She sighed and walked into Wendy's office. She hated that sentence. It spoke of disappointment and bad news.

"I've decided that it would be better for you to ride Quiet Fire in the Pignut Spinney show. I just don't think that Spirit is ready yet."

Kaela's heart sank. She had had big plans for Spirit.

"But what if I put cotton wool in Spirit's ears so he doesn't hear the commotion?"

Wendy looked at her in surprise, "You *want* to ride Spirit?"

"I do."

Wendy put down her pen and stared at Kaela, "Spirit's ears aside, I really think you should ride Quiet Fire on Saturday."

"Why?"

"Because it may be your last time," Wendy said in an odd voice.

Kaela sighed deeply, "Have you sold Quiet Fire?"

Wendy's eyes went wide and the colour drained from her face, "How did you know that?"

Kaela shrugged, "It's a conclusion I have come to based on the evidence presented to me."

"Well yes. Moira is marrying Ben who bought Quiet Fire instead of an engagement ring. They are moving to Johannesburg. They both got better jobs there. If you don't ride him on Saturday, you may never ride him again."

Kaela breathed deeply and nodded. Bart came into the office, walked around his mother's desk, opened a drawer and pulled out a tape measure.

"What are you doing with that?" she asked.

"What do you do with this? Why do you have one?"

"I measure things," she said defensively.

"Well, I have something important to measure," Bart looked at Kaela, "something very important."

Kaela nodded, "I'll go with you."

The two walked off in the direction of the feeding paddock. Wendy stared after them with an odd look on her face.

"What's with the dark cloud over your head?" he asked as they climbed through the fence.

"Your mom just told me that she's sold Quiet Fire."

Bart nodded, "It's sad. He's been here for most of my life."

"He's the only horse I've ridden for the last few years. Wendy says I need to ride him on Saturday because I'll probably never get another chance."

"But what about Spirit?"

Kaela shrugged, "I can't just not ride Quiet Fire. It's not like he's always going to be there."

Bart nodded, then turned to look at her while walking backwards, "But if you had gotten your own horse, would you still be riding Quiet Fire?"

"But Spirit is not my horse."

"No, but he is obviously the next horse in your life."

Kaela grabbed him and pulled him sideways before he walked into a water trough.

"My hero," he said with a laugh.

They walked up to the fallen tree and measured it.

"Five-and-a-quarter feet," he said. "You have already beaten them both."

150

Kaela wasn't surprised. The sight of the jump at the Superius test hadn't frightened her, she had been almost certain she had jumped it before.

"I cheated, I had a taller horse."

Bart smiled, "A taller, *braver* horse."

Kaela looked across the field and remembered herself galloping across it. Spirit's heart had been pounding, he had been excited: he had felt on top of the world too. That was the secret.

Spirit had been a king.

Maybe that was how Time Traveller and Black Satin had managed such unconquerable feats: their riders had understood that these horses were bigger than the riding ring.

Kaela sighed, she wished her mother was around. She wanted her opinion: If anyone could understand Spirit it would have been Felicity.

"Do you ever ask your grandparents for horse-riding advice?" Kaela asked.

Both of Wendy's parents had been professional riders.

"No, I don't talk to them about horses."

"Why not?"

Bart shrugged, "I want to make my own way in life. Their way worked for them, it won't work for me. I want my own way. One that is good enough for me."

Kaela smiled and leaned on the tree, "You don't battle the shadows of your grandparents."

Bart frowned and leaned on the other side, "What do you mean?"

Kaela explained everything that she had learnt about her grandmother.

"And now you feel bogged down? You have to outdo her?"

Kaela shook her head, "Not at all. I feel like the last in this line of amazing women and now I need to do something with this brilliant blood that is flowing through my veins. I feel like they have given me a gift and I'm not using it. In both ways – by neither riding nor writing to challenge myself."

Bart looked just over her shoulder.

"What?" she asked.

"I was looking at Quiet Fire."

Kaela turned to look at him too. She didn't see a horse, she saw her friend.

A friend who would understand that she needed to move on, just as he was doing.

"I think I need to ride Spirit on Saturday."

Bart nodded. She looked at him.

"And even if it doesn't work out like I planned, at least I'll know I tried. And that is all that's important."

"I agree."

"The wolf doesn't care about the opinion of the sheep."

Bart smiled with only one side of his lips, "Does the wolf care about the opinion of another wolf?"

Kaela smiled, "Only if your opinion is a good one."

"I believe you wear your backbone where other people wear their wishbone."

"We'll see on Saturday."

✤ Twelve ✤

Trixie adjusted her Apley Towers tie, kicked the dirt from her knee-length boots and ran her fingers over the iron feather plaited into Siren's tail. With one last look at Apley, she mounted Siren and rode him over to Pignut Spinney. The jumpers were already competing. Both intermediates and advanced competed at the same time, Elizabeth was in the right ring and Warren in the left. The informal scoreboards told Trixie that Apley was in the lead with eleven ribbons. With the added height to the intermediate jumps, very few of those ribbons had come from Trixie's class. The advanced riders from Apley were doing better than ever though: Trixie had never seen them ride so well. They took all three ribbons in all jumping competitions. It had put Apley ahead in general score, but Trixie's class was lagging far behind. If Kaela had been riding Quiet Fire, they would have at least had her ribbons, but for some reason unknown to the kodas,

Kaela had insisted on riding Spirit. Bella, who usually did well in jumping, had been thrown off her game by Gemma's taunting. And Russell always seemed to jeopardise himself for his girlfriend's ill-deserved victory.

Trixie wound her way through the jumpers and made her way to the back ring, where the dressage competitions were being largely ignored by the spectators. The intermediate competitors had yet to win, while Bart and Angela had both won ribbons for the advanced class.

"Listen up Siren, Apley has never brought home an intermediate dressage ribbon. You and I have to change that."

She had no way of knowing if this was Siren's first show, but she was willing to bet it was. Either that or he had had bad experiences at other shows. Siren was not particularly happy to be there. His bottom lip sulked and he kept sighing deeply. She only hoped it wasn't the intense practising that had made him suspicious of the competitor's ring.

"It'll be okay, Siren. We'll be fine."

His ears went back, she leaned forward and tickled him along his tightly braided mane. His ears went to their usual floppy hat stance.

"I suppose in the end we don't have anything to prove to anyone. But I still want to try."

She rode Siren over to the dressage ring and pulled him up next to Vanity Fair. Although they were two different horse breeds, they matched.

"Two little white horses await their turn," Russell said.

Trixie smiled and nodded. She knew Russell shouldn't have bothered waiting for a turn. He was more than likely going to jeopardise himself so that Elizabeth could win. Her name was at the top of the scoreboard. All Russell would have to do was make one mistake. Trixie sighed, she missed the man who used to compete almost at an advanced level, but stayed in the intermediate class because that was where his friends were. Beating Russell in anything had been the highest level of honour because it did not come easily. Now he gave his title away for nothing.

"Do you still believe hearts can only see souls?" Russell asked.

Trixie looked over at him. She had been looking at him for nearly ten years, but had she ever actually seen him before? She knew he had brown hair and eyes. He was a full head taller than her, and when he smiled his eyes crinkled into tiny slits. She had seen that for ages. So why was it that when she looked at him nowadays, she couldn't see any of that? All she could see as she stared at him on his white horse was the freckle on his earlobe. When they were little, they had pretended it was an earring and that he was the stable rebel. His 'rebel' acts had led to him falling during a jump too high for him. He had broken a finger, which still hurt him in the cold. But he said he was lucky that it was on his right hand so it didn't matter. He was the only left-handed rider at Apley. But he had a right-hoofed horse, meaning his wins were even more impressive. He had inherited his dominant left hand from his father who had died three years before. His father had been scared of horses but he had come to every show Russell had ever competed in. Russell never spoke of his father; he choked on the words before he could get them out. The only reason Russell had started liking Trixie was because she had told him that he was the world's most perfect man.

She still believed that.

"Yes, a heart can only see a soul."

"I think so too," he turned in his saddle to look back at the jumping rings.

Where Elizabeth was.

Trixie closed her eyes against the sting of it. She could also see that he purposely lost because making Elizabeth happy made him happy. And, in a weird way, that just made him more perfect.

"Rusty," she said through a heavy croak. He looked back at her, "I want you to know that I am going to try my best to win because Apley Towers has never had an intermediate ribbon. I'm going to try take one back. But if I don't, I want you to know that I tried my best."

"I know. You always try your best," Russell said with a confused frown.

Trixie nodded, "It matters to me that you know that I put my all into it."

Russell smiled, "I know."

"Okay you two, we can hug and kiss later. For now, we have a jerk to beat," said Bella as she rode up to them.

She pointed to the ring where Gemma rode Empire Gold.

"I don't care about bringing a ribbon home, we just need to make sure she doesn't," Bella said.

"Would you have us destroy her round?" Russell asked.

Bella turned on him, *"No,* just ride better than her."

"Up next," the announcer said, "is Sibella Matthews on Kapella Pony."

Bella nudged KaPoe into the ring and gave what Trixie believed to be her best ever dressage routine. She made no mistakes and smiled deceptively sweetly to the judges at the end. Russell and Trixie cheered loudly as Bella's name replaced Gemma's at the number two spot.

"You know we are going to go back to hating her tomorrow right?" Russell said.

"Let's give her until Monday."

The next rider was good enough to knock Bella down into third place. And the rider after that knocked her down to fourth. She didn't care. She had set out to beat Gemma, and that was what she had done.

Trixie sighed to see that Elizabeth was still at the top.

"Beatrix King on Siren's Song."

Trixie looked at Russell, "Remember, I tried my hardest to get Apley a ribbon."

He nodded.

She nudged Siren into the ring. Her heart beat in her ears.

Cheering from the crowd made her look over. Angela, Kaela, Björn and Finley had all made it over to watch her round. She turned back to make sure that Russell was watching her.

He was.

She stopped in front of the judges table, saluted them, and began.

Despite his displeasure at the show, Siren responded to her every aid. But Trixie couldn't concentrate. Her mind kept wandering. There had been a competition exactly like this one before. Both Russell and Trixie had placed nowhere. She had later found him in Apley's feeding paddock, on the fallen tree. At first she had thought he was crying over his loss, but that had been the furthest thing from his mind. The competition had been the first that his father had not attended. Trixie hadn't known what to say. She had simply sat next to him, watching the sun disappear behind the oak trees. The ones that surrounded the property and kept Apley – and all those in it – safe from harm.

Trixie forgot the next move: she had no idea where she was in the routine. The judges stared at her, their eyes reflecting her falling marks. Her vision blurred, she blinked back her tears.

She had two choices, fail or fail spectacularly.

In that moment, Trixie chose to be splendid and own the ring. She nudged Siren into a piaffe. Then, she dropped her reins and stirrups and took him around the ring with her arms crossed, as though in a sulk that Siren had messed

up the routine. She took him up to a canter, clapped and half-halted him. The crowd laughed. She clapped and half-halted him again. They laughed again. She clapped one last time and he came to a complete stop. She pretended she didn't know what he was doing. Siren, joining in the game, swung his head back and forth as though saying 'no'. For good measure he even stuck his tongue out at the crowd. They laughed loudly. Siren neighed at them. His ears perked forward and he happily awaited the next instruction. Trixie clapped several times then put her hands on her hips in a huff. Then she pretended to discover her reins. She picked them up, showed them to the crowd who laughed loudly. She then hooked her one leg on the pommel, shook the reins and rode out of the ring side saddle. She came back in, saluted the judges and went back out again.

The crowd stood up and cheered loudly. It was the first time that day that dressage had actually been interesting.

"Well that was different," Russell said with a smile.

Trixie shrugged, "I forgot the routine."

She saw the judges tearing up her scorecard, and tears came to her eyes again. Well, her first show with Siren had been a complete disaster.

"Apley doesn't get a ribbon," she whispered.

"The last dressage rider of the day is Russell Drover on Vanity Fair."

Russell turned to look back at Elizabeth, then looked at Trixie. She had the heels of her hands buried in her eyes, trying to remove any evidence of tears.

Russell looked back at Elizabeth, then nudged Vanity Fair into a walk.

"Hey Beatrix Bunny, remember I tried my best too."

He went into the ring.

He saluted the judges.

He presented a flawless routine.

Russell stopped in front of the judge's table and smiled as all five of them gave him a perfect score of ten. Russell's name replaced Elizabeth's on the number one spot.

"From what I hear, this will be the first time Apley Towers takes an intermediate dressage ribbon home," the announcer said.

The kodas, Björn and Finley cheered loudly. As Russell rode past, he held up his hand for a high five. Trixie leaned over and gave him one, nearly falling out of the saddle of course. But she didn't really care.

Apley finally had a dressage ribbon from the intermediates, and that was all that mattered.

Trixie indicated to the kodas that she was taking Siren back to Apley. They nodded and waved her off. She didn't want to stay to see Russell be presented with a ribbon that Elizabeth had expected. She wanted to remember the look on his face when he won for Apley, not the look when he explained why he hadn't let Elizabeth win.

She trotted Siren down the road and back to his stall, where she dismounted him, led him in and began untacking him. She would leave the plaits in his mane and tail until they fell out on their own. She liked him looking so professional, even if he didn't.

"Why don't you like shows?" she asked him, "Or do you? You just don't like the amount of pressure I put on you."

She stroked his long, sleek neck. He closed his eyes and sighed in pleasure.

"You seemed to enjoy yourself when we were playing. Do you like freestyle dressage? Or did you just like me playing with you instead of demanding things?"

"I think it's the last one," Russell said as he led Vanity Fair into his stall.

The blue ribbon waved from her bridle.

The blue ribbon Trixie had hoped to have on Siren's bridle.

Russell began untacking Vanity Fair. He put the ribbon on the floor outside the stall, and took the equipment to the tack room. Trixie left Siren's stall and went to pick it up.

It was blue and white with Pignut Spinney's emblem in the face. The streamers said 'Dressage' and 'First Place' in gold letters.

She wished that she had won it.

"It's only a ribbon, Trix," Russell said as he came back with his grooming kit.

"I know," she said sadly.

Did she?

Russell spun on her.

"Why are you suddenly so into winning ribbons? When

have you ever cared before? You used to show off about being the only one at Apley that could get Slow-Moe to gallop. *That* was your ribbon. Now all you care about is winning a piece of over-fluffed up fabric. What happened?"

"I need to show people that Siren was the best choice for me." She quickly held up her hand before Russell could interrupt her, "Yes, I know that it shouldn't matter what other people think. I know, but it does matter. I need them to see that Siren is my perfect match."

"I was going to say that it does matter what some people think. But those people already know that Siren is perfect for you. A ribbon is not going to make any difference."

Trixie sighed deeply. Something in her recognised these words. They had been whispered at the back of her mind whenever her eyes closed at night. She had ignored them.

"You don't need ribbons to prove you are good enough," he said.

That had been whispered to her too.

"Ribbons don't mean anything. They are just hard work for an over-glorified piece of fabric. I was not having fun out there. Neither was Vanity Fair. The pressure to get that ribbon was unreal, and it wasn't fun. Riding is supposed to be fun, or what's the point?"

"If you think that then why get the ribbon? Apley would have been fine without it."

Russell sighed deeply, "Because you wanted one for Apley."

She closed her eyes and blocked him out. If he no longer wanted her, she couldn't let him in. Not even when he had won a ribbon just for her.

Russell walked into his stall and began grooming Vanity Fair. Trixie didn't know what to say. She pulled the streamers through her fingers.

He was right, it was just fabric.

"I've never seen you cry over a competition either. I've seen you land up underneath the horse and you still didn't cry. I had to rebuild the jump after you went nose first into the pole. Your nose was broken, and you still didn't cry. Today you cry because you forgot one of the most stupid routines I've ever come across. Why? What happened? Where is Trixie?"

She closed her eyes and breathed in. She didn't know. Had this happened a year ago, she would have laughed her head off at the experience and already been back at Pignut Spinney supporting her friends. She wouldn't be looking longingly at a ribbon won by someone who hadn't enjoyed winning it.

"Trixie is gone," she said, "she's too bogged down by everyone."

"By who?" Russell asked without looking at her.

She sighed, "By everyone. Angela is practically famous. Did you see her on TV this morning? They made it out that she was a gigantic hero for not winning. Imagine if she had won! Kaela is suddenly being trusted to train a stallion. Bart

166

is about to compete in the Empire Games. Finley can beat the unbeatable Angela if he really tries. Even Bella is doing well. Where does that leave Trixie? Nowhere! Or at least, it leaves her talking about herself in the third person."

"You never cared before," he said without looking at her, "loving what you were doing was enough."

"Well I care now."

"And yet, before, you were happy and now you are miserable."

She couldn't argue that.

Russell sighed, "Women are just such hard work."

Trixie snorted as she thought of the men in her life. They were exhausting. If she wasn't juggling her feelings for Finley with her grief over the loss of her friendship with Russell, she was trying to keep everyone happy. She even seemed to be walking on eggshells to keep her father happy lately. And Leo had had to silence her twice the week before. The men in her life were just never satisfied with anything.

Especially Russell and Finley.

"Men are hard work too," she said.

"We are not. Give us food and we are happy. We don't even need clean clothes."

"Eww."

Russell laughed. It was a good sound. She couldn't remember the last time she had heard it. Maybe he was bogged down too.

"Who is hard work?" she asked.

"Everyone! All my female friends, Elizabeth, Wendy, even my mom is hard work. I miss the days when no one expected anything from me. When I was invisible. When the library didn't even register that I brought my books back."

"Am I hard work?"

Russell turned to face her, she waited for him to confirm that she was indeed the hardest of all the females to please.

He shook his head, "No." Then he pointed to the ribbon, "Well you were when I had to win that thing for you. But actually, you are the only person who never tires me out. Generally you just leave me alone until I need a shoulder to lean on, then you are there."

"And you *like* that?"

Russell shrugged, "It's comforting. It means I don't have to go around pleasing you."

That was not what she'd expected to hear. She thought Russell would confess what a miserable friend she was. Or how she was usually the one to give him a reason to find a shoulder.

Russell turned back to Vanity Fair and loosened her plaits.

"Am I a good shoulder?" Trixie asked.

"The best."

So why did I get replaced? She wanted to ask.

But she already knew. It was because she had taken the jewel for granted. She had learnt the hard way that hearts can only see souls. It doesn't matter what the eyes see, you are not led by your eyes.

Humans follow their hearts.

She had learnt, far too late, that Russell was not just good enough.

He was the best.

She walked forward and gave him his ribbon, "Thank you for winning it. Apley finally has a rosette for intermediate dressage."

"The world is right again," he said sarcastically, and took it.

The wind blew through Apley Towers, cold and loud. It brought winter on its tail. The oak trees rustled around the property. In the silence Trixie could hear the ocean. It was high tide. The dune she and Siren had climbed a week ago was probably underwater by this point. How strange was it that the very coast line could change around you. Not even maps were set in stone.

"Do you believe people can suddenly change?"

"Nope. I think change takes a lot of work. And even if you do change overnight it is an act. You'll soon get tired of who you changed into."

She put her head down on her crossed arms. The stall door creaked under this new pressure.

Joseph walked past with two horses, "The passion that burns brightly and unexpectedly burns itself out just as quickly, and all that you are left with is the blackened stump of exhaustion."

Trixie closed her eyes and tried to think of all the things

that she had suddenly felt passionate about: winning blue to prove she didn't need jumping; proving that she was super-intelligent at astrophysics to make up for the fact that the rest of the kodas were all doing so much better than her; her romance with Finley.

She looked up at Russell, he stared off into the distance.

Trixie closed her eyes and buried her face in her arms again. She had wanted to win blue because she had it in her head that blue ribbons equalled an acceptance from everyone that she was right in all her decisions. But no one really ever bothered with her decisions. In reality, she just needed someone to tell her that her decisions were good enough.

She needed to tell herself this. And believe it.

And as for the other kodas doing well, that wasn't new. They had always done well. Trixie had suddenly turned everything into a competition. Each koda knew she was good enough. Trixie had simply forgotten this.

As for Finley, she knew the reason she had kept her kiss a secret. It was simply that she wasn't interested in a relationship with him. Phoenix and Angela had pushed her so much that she had forgotten that she was never really interested in relationships with anyone. She got a crush on someone, admired them for a while and then moved on. At the beginning of the year she had been completely enamoured with Warren, and then it had been Satyr. Finley had simply been next on the list. That was the way she liked it. She had no time for boyfriends. But Phoenix and Angela didn't understand that. They didn't know that a crush was simply a crush and nothing more. Trixie had let herself get carried away on their excitement. Now that she thought about it, Kaela had never questioned the friendship with Finley: she knew that it was only a matter of time before Trixie found someone new to drool over.

Joseph was right, all these quick passions had done nothing but left her confused, irritated, and above all, exhausted. She had confused what she wanted, with what other people wanted for her.

Russell sighed loudly. Maybe he had come to the same conclusion.

"It's the passion that is slow and quiet, and comes while you aren't looking that lasts the longest," Joseph said as he walked back. "That's the passion that changes lives and energises the world."

Trixie stared after him, "I'm starting to agree with Kaela: Joseph is psychic."

Russell raced over to the door, "Hey Joe, do you know the lottery numbers?"

Trixie laughed. It was like a release of tension. The need to be better than everyone else, instead of good enough for herself flowed out of her and into the wind where it was taken out to sea.

Trixie didn't miss it.

Angela gave one last cheer for the riders and stood up to leave.

"I've got to get Dawn warmed up," she said to Björn.

"Want me to come with you?"

Angela sighed – he was offering to be her bodyguard in case she ran into Gemma. Was that really the world she wanted? Where people had to constantly stand between her and her problems?

"No, go support Bart for a while."

She walked off the property, down the road and into Apley. It wasn't deserted. There were a few riders exercising horses in the free rings. They weren't all Apley riders either.

Angela loved that. Apley Towers and its neighbouring school were technically rivals, but they pulled together and acted as a unit when they needed to. Sagittarius Stables would never have allowed riders from other schools to use their equipment. They barely allowed Angela to do anything, simply because she was privately tutored.

It was becoming more and more clear every day of her life that she had made the right choice by switching to Apley Towers.

"In retrospect, destiny always looks like a well-made choice," Joseph said as he took beginner horses back to their stall.

Angela frowned, she couldn't quite tell if Joseph was saying that Apley was her destiny or just a good choice.

The sight of the camera crew filming the stable brought other thoughts to her mind: It had been Gemma who had eventually pushed Angela to find a new stable. Gemma had purposely darted across the practice ring while Angela had been warming Dawn up. The frightened horse had reared up, throwing Angela to the ground. Dawn had bolted away from Gemma, and her leg had come straight down onto Angela's stomach. She had been rushed to hospital to check for internal bleeding. There hadn't been any, but the nail on Dawn's hoof had caught Angela's skin and ripped a long line across her stomach. She still had the scar. Angela hadn't been able to compete for weeks, but that hadn't bugged her. Gemma's laughter as she fell had reverberated across her mind and made the decision for her. She would find a new stable.

And now here she was, cosy at Apley. Safe from harm, with good friends and even a boyfriend. Not to mention, two articles under her belt as well as two TV interviews.

She looked across Apley Towers, from the tall oak trees to Wendy's two chimney pots. The three riding rings, the stalls, the buildings and the creek. Her paradise.

Her destiny.

Joseph walked back past her, "Destiny only takes you so far. Sheer hard work gets you the rest of the way."

He was right. She had been given opportunities, but she had been the one to take them.

She had created her own destiny.

"Ah, just the woman we want to see!" a boisterous man cried as he walked up to Angela.

"Hi Gary," she said to the show producer.

"We have all of our establishing shots. The only thing left to do now is see you ride and hopefully – fingers crossed – take a ribbon, we'll interview you before and after. You okay with all that?"

"Of course."

"Brilliant. We watched the clip of you on Horse Masters this morning. I can't pretend to know anything about horses, but that was a good interview. I mean you resigned, someone else won, but you still came out on top. Must have been a great feeling."

"Yes, putting my horse first is more important than ribbons."

"So you said on the show."

"Because I meant it: then and now. Dawn wouldn't have handled that jump, she would have crashed right through it, and I will never know what psychological damage that would have done to her. My horse comes first."

"And that is why you will go far in this business," Gary said, "Because in your mind, success is not winning, it's your relationship with your horse. That means you can never lose."

"Are you a motivational speaker?" Angela asked with a frown.

"No, I just see things that other people choose to ignore.

How do you think I pick the people I interview?"

"Uhm … I don't know."

"What did I tell you about saying 'uhm'?" he asked with a smile, "As soon as I read your first article, where you said your greatest accomplishment was winning a scavenger hunt, even though you're the three-time Equestrian International champion, I knew you were perfect for my show. You understand what is really important. Don't change. Most of the world has to remind themselves to be like you."

Angela nodded, "What would you do if bullies constantly tried to bring you down?"

Gary smiled, "Unfortunately those who are different, smarter, more talented, and more determined will always be attacked by those too scared to be different too. Don't bother with them. You feed their fires by engaging in their fight. You don't have to attend every battle you are invited to."

Angela left them then to get Dawn warmed up and over to Pignut Spinney. She thought about what Gary had said.

He was right, she could never lose.

The camera followed her the entire time. She waited her turn outside the advanced ring and spoke to Gary whenever he asked a question. She had to breathe deeply before each answer and think clearly about what she wanted to say. Gary only seemed to ask questions that made Angela seem like a super-equestrian. She wasn't comfortable with this: she remembered being younger, watching professional riders and just being intimidated. She wanted aspiring riders to know that Angela wasn't perfect, she wasn't a superstar.

Eventually she said, "I'm not always the best at everything. All of the people here are amazing, wonderful riders. And they don't let the opinion of other people bring them down. Most of the time." With that, Angela smiled and made her way over to the competition ring.

Angela won blue and it was caught on camera. She looked sadly at the scoreboard, Bart's name wasn't up there. She didn't know why he hadn't competed, but it hadn't been the same without their playful banter.

It was only when she was putting Dawn back in the stall that she saw Bart and Björn carrying poles and foam bricks over to Pignut Spinney.

"What are they doing?"

She gave each of her horses one last pat and followed the boys.

"Hello Angela May," a cold voice said, "I noticed that you only won three blues today?"

Angela smiled thinly and turned to Gemma.

"I figured I would give other, *lesser* riders a chance," she spat.

Instead of putting Gemma down, this only seemed to give her strength.

"Oh, I am so glad you think that Trixie and Kaela are lesser riders."

Angela sighed, there was no way to win an argument

against Gemma. No matter what she could say, Gemma would twist it and keep coming. Angela was simply fuelling the fire. Gemma only responded to strength, and sometimes that strength was simply to walk away.

"Have a good day, Gemma. Go take care of your horse, he deserves love."

Angela turned and walked away.

"Coward!" Gemma called, "You are so scared of me. It's totally pathetic. No wonder you had to run away from my stable."

Angela smiled and walked to Pignut Spinney. She'd let Bella deal with Gemma in future. Bella seemed to enjoy it.

And maybe, just maybe, they were both as equally insecure as each other. And that was why they were so mean.

Angela stopped for a moment and breathed in the wind coming from Apley. It smelt of the mountains and winter. It was headed towards the ocean. For the first time in a long time, she felt invincible. There was no one who could get her down.

She knew she was good enough.

And it didn't matter what anyone else thought.

And maybe that truly was the secret of success. If you were strong from the inside, nothing could break you down.

She smiled and strutted off to Pignut Spinney, the sun shining brightly on her shoulders and the melody of the wind in her ears. In a few hours the curtain opened on Phoenix's play. Angela stopped again, breathed deeply and sent good vibes across the Atlantic to her friend.

"Good luck, Phoenix. If anyone can do it, it's you."

With that she and her shadow walked off.

Kaela breathed deeply. It was almost time.

She had spotted Bart and Björn with the jump. They had each given her a thumbs up. This had only made her more nervous.

Things had not gone well for her that day. She could forget ribbons: she hadn't even managed to finish a course. Spirit was simply not ready for competitions. But that was okay, he now had the experience. He knew what was expected of him next time, and that was more important. As a last resort, Kaela had taken him through the beginners' course. It was half the size, and the jumps were barely off the ground. In fact, they were so low that Spirit had simply trotted over them. But he now had the experience of finishing a course. Kaela had made such a fuss of him when he crossed the finish line that he hadn't wanted to move from it.

Kaela had also been given a 'Clear Round' ribbon, something she hadn't received since moving up to the intermediate level. The Fairies had cheered loudly for Spirit, another thing he had enjoyed. He had nickered loudly at them with what looked like a smile on his face.

The next time Spirit was taken into a competitor's ring,

he would remember how good it felt to finish.

"Kae," Bart said as he walked up, "I've spoken to the dude with the microphone, he'll make the announcement in half an hour."

Kaela smiled, thanked him and put her 'Clear Round' rosette in her blazer pocket. She looked around at the gathered spectators. Her father and Niamh were on the grandstand. This was the first competition her father had attended in years. The joke, of course, was that she had achieved only one 'Clear Round' ribbon. Not unlike the competitions he used to watch when she was still a beginner. Trixie's parents as well as Russell's mother were there too. What was it about this specific competition that had brought them all to the spectators' stand?

Perhaps there was something in the air.

Björn waved from the other end of the school and pointed to the announcer's table. Kaela's stomach flipped over.

There was no going back now.

"Ladies and gentlemen," the announcer said, "we have had a fabulous competition today, with many winners. All riders and horses have done incredibly well. The owners of Pignut Spinney would like to thank everyone who helped, competed, and supported. Give yourselves a round of applause."

A burst of applause erupted across the stands.

"Before I can officially end the competition, I need to make one more announcement," he paused to gather his papers. "Apparently we have one rider who wants to challenge the outdated rules of competition."

The crowd gasped. Out of the corner of her eye, Kaela could see her father look from the announcer to his daughter.

"Oh he knows me so well," she said to her shadow. The shadow almost seemed to nod.

"Kaela Willoughby would like to challenge the Superius test."

She smiled at the confused expressions in the crowd.

"You want to challenge the test?" Derrick asked, "The actual test?"

Kaela shook her head, "I want to challenge the rules of the test. Angela didn't jump five feet, but then neither did Gemma. She won by default because the rules fell in her favour."

Gemma and Ms Larkin scowled at her.

"Are you kidding?" Gemma snorted "You can't talk, you haven't got that miserable horse to do *anything* today. I've beaten both you and Trixie in *everything*."

Kaela shrugged, "Spirit and Siren are simply too big for the ring."

"Spirit and Siren are too big for the ring," Gemma mocked in a shrill voice, "What does that even mean?"

"You will never know because you don't understand what it means to be a real rider."

"Except for the fact that I keep winning."

Kaela sighed, you couldn't argue with Gemma. It was

180

like playing chess with a pigeon. No matter how good your moves are, the pigeon will still hop on the board, knock over the pieces and strut around like it has won.

She looked over at Gemma, "I don't expect you to understand, but I'm going to bring the blue ribbon to Apley … symbolically."

"How?" Gemma spat.

Kaela gestured to Bart and Björn, "They will build the jump to five feet and I'll take Spirit over it. I'm not going to argue with you, Gemma. I'm riding for myself and for Apley, a riding school who teaches us to understand our horses rather than just order them around. I'm going to show you a true horse and rider partnership."

Gemma smirked, "And when you knock that wall down? What have you shown us then?"

Kaela shrugged, "That I've tried to do something great and even if I failed, I was good enough."

She didn't stand around to hear what Gemma had to say, she nudged Spirit into a trot and took him to the jump. She allowed him to sniff it and take a good look at it. Bart had set the jump up in line with the ring fence. No one had noticed.

He came over, pulled her foot out of the stirrup, put his foot in and pulled himself up. He brought his lips up to her ear and whispered, "You are the last in an impressive line of women. Their blood pumps in your veins. Show them what you are made of."

"Wear my backbone where others wear their wishbone?"

"And gallop where warriors fear to tread."

He jumped down and smiled at her. She smiled back.

"You got this, Miss Kae."

"I know."

Kaela smiled at her and trotted Spirit away from the jump.

Gemma scowled, "Let's see her get that fleabag over that jump. She hasn't even gotten him over three feet. Forget five."

Kaela smiled and cantered Spirit around the ring.

"You are going to wear him out," Russell called.

Kaela shook her head, she needed his heart pumping, she needed him to feel as though he rode the back of the wind.

She needed him to think he was a king.

"Oh please just hurry up and do us all the favour of jumping so we can all see you fail," Gemma said once the boys were out of the way.

Bart came back into the ring and put something on top of the jump, in the right corner. Kaela smiled when she saw it.

The bottled moonlight.

Bart smiled and walked out of the ring. It was almost as though he had left an enchantment with the moonlight behind him.

A spell to get Spirit to fly.

Kaela turned Spirit around and jumped him over the ring fence.

"She's quitting," Gemma cried.

"No, she's not," Bart said.

Kaela galloped Spirit down to the end of the school, halted and turned him. He stood, his ears perked, ready and waiting.

"Listen up, Spirit, once upon a time in a land far, far away, a powerful priestess rode a wonderful horse. They were brave and true to themselves. They took double gold in the Empire Games. That priestess was my mother and that horse was your cousin. Let's show them that we are worthy of those titles."

Spirit neighed loudly. She looked down at their shadows. There was no difference between her and Spirit, and Felicity and Black Satin … they were one in the same.

"And if we don't make it we are still good enough, simply because we tried."

Spirit stomped his right hoof, Kaela signalled that she was about to jump. She nudged Spirit into a gallop. He sprang forward, they raced down the track, jumped the fence, and raced on. The crowd gasped as one. Spirit lifted off the ground, Kaela leaned forward and looked at the bottled moonlight.

The two of them flew.

Spirit landed on the other side with a thump. Everyone in the stable cheered. Spirit gave a little buck in answer to them.

"Ouch," Kaela said as she snapped forward. She hadn't expected that.

She halted him and turned to look at the jump.

It still stood.

She had done it.

She had understood how Spirit worked, and had adapted herself to his ways.

They had worked in perfect harmony.

And that was what being a horse rider was all about.

That was how she and Spirit proved to themselves that they were good enough.

A Silver Lining for the Lost Kodas

Dear Phoenix,
Here's the review from the newspaper.

Last night's play, The Battle for Bellatrix, was above and beyond what I expected from a high school play. The heroine, Stella, is spirited away to another planet in order to save the star, Bellatrix. The script was cleverly written. The sets were spellbinding. The acting was on the subtle side, adopting a refreshing 'less is more' attitude. This, I think, suited such a script more than normal stage acting would have. The all Native Canadian cast and crew came together to create a truly memorable piece, which I could easily see on any stage anywhere in the world. I was even more surprised to find that the writer herself was playing lead role. She did this with such flair that I was left wondering if the next great star had already been born. Although, her onstage kiss with the spaceship driver seemed to surprise the actor more than the audience. All in all, a truly brilliant play. The White Feather twins have outdone themselves.

Not bad for a first-timer. Can't wait to see you tonight. Rowan.

P.S. The surprise kiss was my favourite part of the play. Glad it made the review.

Dear Miss Beatrix King

We managed to catch your rather scintillating dressage routine at Pignut Spinney last week. We were rather disappointed when the judges refused to score you and Siren's Song.

Your freestyled routine showed us what a marvellous relationship you have with your horse. Indeed, Siren seemed to be playing along with you. It reminded us of the freestyle routines done by Felicity Willoughby all those years ago.

You are quite the intriguing rider, and we would be exceptionally privileged if you accepted our invitation to compete at Equestrian International.

Our stable will be breaking new ground in the

A STELLAR
PERFORMANCE

coming months, as we will be the first to host an entirely freestyled dressage show.

We would very much like you and Siren's Song to represent Apley Towers at the first of these shows.

We look forward to your reply.

Sincerely,

Shannon and Cecilia Michaels, and the rest of the Equestrian International team.

P.S. Didn't Siren's Song used to live with us? I'm sure I recognise him.

Dear Kaela,

When I first met your grandmother she told me that she enjoyed the work of Jerome K. Jerome, especially his book Three Men in a Boat. As you noticed, I am an avid collector of signed books, and one of the first that I purchased was Three Men in a Boat which Mr Jerome had dedicated to a friend of his. I had always wanted to give it to your grandmother as Jerome's writing did for her what her writing did for me. But I never got around to it … I always thought there would be more time. So instead, I am sending the book to you. Treasure it: your grandmother learned everything she knew about writing from it. Perhaps it will teach you something too. You are so much like her. She was brave and kind, just like you.

Regards,

Anthony Henry.

P.S. I have returned the cheque. Be a dear and give it to that woman. And tell her to keep her donkey away from my begonias.

P.P.S. The first rule of writing is that there are only three rules of writing, but no one knows what they are. Good luck.

Dear Miss Angela May.

We, at Horse Masters, have been keeping a close watch on your horse-riding career so far and are quite impressed with all you have done and your beliefs concerning the happiness of your horse. Your decision to resign at the Superius test for the sake of your horse made quite an impression on us.

It is with great pleasure that we invite you to host your own three-part TV show.

We would, of course, want to film almost exclusively at Apley Towers and show the viewer what it means to be a true horse rider. This would involve filming all your friends too: your companionship with them is so very important. You are very lucky you are to have these people around you.

After your stunning performance at the Superius test and your interview on Sports Masters (plus a great review from Gary), we feel that there is no one better suited to teach South Africa what competitive riders are really made of.

You are an inspiration to future riders.

Sincerely,

The team at Horse Masters.